# THE GHOST RIDERS

Center Point
Large Print

# THE GHOST RIDERS

Philip Ketchum

CENTER POINT LARGE PRINT
THORNDIKE, MAINE

This Center Point Large Print edition
is published in the year 2024 by arrangement with
Golden West Inc.



Originally published in the US by Ace Books.

The text of this Large Print edition is unabridged.
In other aspects, this book may vary
from the original edition.
Printed in the United States of America
on permanent paper sourced using
environmentally responsible foresting methods.
Set in 16-point Times New Roman type.

ISBN 979-8-89164-244-7 (hardcover)
ISBN 979-8-89164-248-5 (paperback)

The Library of Congress has cataloged this record
under Library of Congress Control Number: 2024935909

# CAST OF CHARACTERS

**Johnny Lang**
Marked for death, he had only the ghost of a chance to survive.

**Ben Mohegan**
He put his trust in just one thing—a bullwhip.

**Dru Mohegan**
She wanted vengeance, but not bloodshed.

**Pache Yates**
Half Indian—and all killer.

**Rich Gilmore**
He moved at night and lied by day.

**Syl Mohegan**
A dancehall girl who refused to sing for her supper.

# THE GHOST RIDERS

# I

The cave was well screened with shrubbery. Its narrow opening was in an almost inaccessible point on the climbing face of a cliff. On the third day of the search, some of the members of the posse from Georgia City explored a number of the lower caves, but no one climbed as high as the one in which Johnny Lang was hiding.

Toward sundown, and as the posse rode away, Johnny hoped he had seen the last of them, but he wasn't at all sure. The persistence of the searchers was surprising. If they had kept on the job for three days, they might continue for a fourth day. Or a fifth. And that posed a problem. He was short of rations, short of water. He couldn't stay where he was much longer.

After the posse left, Johnny crawled to the mouth of the cave. Then, through the screening shrubbery, he studied the valley below. Nowhere could he see any movement. Of course, someone could have been left behind, hidden in the trees—someone to stand watch. But he doubted if that had happened. These Pothole Hills were honeycombed with caves. It was no more realistic for the posse to believe that he was hiding near here, than to think he was hiding somewhere else.

Still scanning the trees in the valley below,

Johnny considered what lay ahead. After dark, water would be no problem. He could climb down to the creek below—and climb back. But that didn't take care of food. Or a horse. If he was to make good his escape, he had to get a horse. The one he had ridden into the hills, he had lost. Possibly, if he left shortly after dark and made an all-night hike through the hills, he could get down to Macey's ranch on Crows' Bench, well before dawn. There, Carl Macey might sell him a horse—but he couldn't be sure. It was five years since he had seen him, and sometimes, men change. That was one of the bitter truths Johnny had learned.

He scowled through the shrubbery, deciding it had been a mistake to return to Georgia City. What had happened, of course, had been an accident. He had come back, meaning to stay only a day or so. He had wanted to see Merth, and Rich Gilmore. He had wanted to bury some private ghosts of the past. He hadn't meant to run counter to Ben Mohegan, but that was the way things worked out.

Johnny sighed. He thought of the night-long hike through the hills. It wouldn't be easy on him. It would be up and down most of the way and the boots he was wearing weren't made for such work. In addition to that, he couldn't be sure of his welcome at Macey's, but he would worry about that later.

A sound outside startled him. It was the dislodging of a rock, and it might have been accidental—or it might not. From the edge of the cave he couldn't see the face of the cliff. It wasn't easy to climb up here—but he had made it, and someone else could have done it. Johnny reached for his gun, then lay listening. A faint, scraping sound reached his ears. It was off to the left. He heard it again—the brushing of a boot against the hard earth. *Someone was outside, climbing toward him. And he wasn't far off.*

"Johnny!" a voice called. "Johnny Lang! If you're up there, say so. I've got to see you. This is Rich Gilmore."

Some of the tension which had gripped Johnny's body slid away. But not all of it. What was Rich Gilmore doing out there? Had he been with the posse, or had he come here independently? Once, five years ago, he and Rich had been close friends. They might have stayed friends if it hadn't been for Merth. Or possibly, they still were friends. He just didn't know. The brief and uncomfortable meeting they had had in Georgia City had been hard to analyze.

"Johnny, can't you hear me?" Rich called. "Merth was sure this was where I'd find you. I've got to see you."

Johnny checked his gun, then holstered it. It was a hell of a thing if he couldn't trust a man like Rich. He crawled forward and stood up, still partially behind the shrubbery. And he made an answer. "Sure. Here I am, Rich. You alone?"

"All alone, Johnny. The posse rode back to Macey's. Plan to spend the night there, then continue the search in the morning."

"Then it wouldn't have been smart if I'd have walked to Macey's."

"Not too smart. They'd have had you."

Rich Gilmore was on a narrow, climbing ledge, a little below the cave opening. He was a rather stocky man, thick bodied but not fat. He had ruddy cheeks, very black hair, and he wore a black mustache. Like Johnny, he had been reared on a ranch, but after his schooling he had gone to work with Judge Elliott, reading law, and now was a fully accredited lawyer. In the black business suit he was wearing, he looked out of place standing on the face of the cliff.

"Want to climb up?" Johnny asked. "Or should we climb down. You don't look comfortable, pinned against the side of a mountain."

"I'm not," Rich answered. "I've climbed about as far as I could, and I'm in favor of turning back. It's getting dark, too. This could be a mean climb in the darkness."

"Then we'll go down," Johnny said. "Take it easy."

He followed Rich Gilmore down the ledge, and on the way, Johnny decided he knew why Rich was here. Merth had prompted the trip. Once, she and Johnny had planned on being married. Then, he had been sent to prison, and while he was away, Merth found a substitute—Rich Gilmore. But she still felt guilty. She felt she owed something to Johnny and here was a way to pay him: help him escape. Down at the foot of the cliff, Rich undoubtedly would offer him a horse, some supplies—and maybe even some money.

Johnny's scowl grew deeper. Unreasonably, he didn't like what was happening. He needed help, but he didn't like being paid off.

From the foot of the cliff they walked to the fringing trees, where Rich had tied his horse, and if he had brought a second animal, Johnny couldn't see it. He turned to look curiously at Rich Gilmore.

"We've a little time," Rich said. "Might as well sit down. I don't think we'll be interrupted, and anyhow, we've got to talk."

"I'm not much good at talking," Johnny said.

"A little won't hurt," Rich said. "Are you interested in the man you shot—Will Mohegan?"

"Yes. How badly was he hurt?"

"They say he's dying."

Johnny shook his head. "I fired high. I hit him in the shoulder. It couldn't have been that serious."

"I don't think it is serious," Rich said. "Will Mohegan was taken home. The doctor's been there, several times. He told me, in confidence, that the man will recover. But the story going around is that he'll die. Ben Mohegan is responsible for that. If people think Will Mohegan is dying, then the men searching for you have an excuse for shooting you down. Afterwards, Will Mohegan can recover, through some miracle."

"And I can thank Ben Mohegan for that."

"He's always hated you, Johnny. He hated your father. You stood against him, every chance you had. It isn't a smart thing to get in the way of Ben Mohegan."

"And this Will Mohegan—who's he? I never heard of him before."

"He's a nephew."

"He started the fight in town. I tried to dodge it, but couldn't."

"Will's like that. He's a little man and he's trying to make himself an image of his uncle. It would have been a deep notch in his gun if he could have killed one of his uncle's enemies."

Johnny sat down, resting on a fallen log. He shook his head. "I've been away five years, Rich. I didn't come back to stay. My people are dead. The old ranch has been sold. I've no roots left in this part of the country. Years ago, I fought against Ben Mohegan, but I've no interest in him now."

Rich was staring at him intently. "You mean that, Johnny?"

"Yes."

"You have no more hatred for Ben Mohegan?"

"It's an old hatred, Rich. It's like an old love. It's part of the past and if I feel it at all, it's no more than a dull ache. It doesn't really hurt."

Rich flushed uncomfortably. He looked away, and for the moment, was silent.

Johnny let the silence continue. He thought briefly of Merth, then turned his mind to what had happened in Georgia City, four days before. After a short talk with Rich, he had headed to the saloon for a drink—and he had felt he needed it. He didn't get to finish it, however. A brash young man had broken in on his silence, and had driven him to the point of defending himself. In every way he could, he had tried to avoid it. But he had failed, and at the end of an ugly scene, he had dropped Will Mohegan with a bullet in the shoulder.

Rich cleared his throat. He said, "Johnny, did you mean what you said a few minutes ago? How do you feel about Ben Mohegan?"

"How do I feel about him?" Johnny repeated. "Actually, I don't know. Suppose I put it this way. He's an unpleasant memory."

"He stirred up the posse which has been chasing you."

"I had been planning to leave, anyhow. And I got away, Rich. Or at least, I haven't yet been caught."

"Men who have been in prison, usually are bitter."

"Bitter? Sure I'm bitter. But more at myself than anyone else. Ben Mohegan bought a blooded bull we had hoped to buy. I knew his representatives were going to the sale, and were going to overbid us. I tried to prevent it by holding up the man representing Mohegan—and I was arrested for what I tried. It was a foolish thing to do. I blame myself for what I did."

Rich nodded slowly. "Johnny, I came here to outline three propositions," he said. "In view of what you've said, I imagine you're interested in only one."

"And what is that."

"I've an extra horse down valley, about a mile from here. I tied the horse there when the climb got difficult. You can have the horse and ride away. The saddle bags hold a week's ration of food stuffs. I can loan you some money, too. It can be repaid, anytime in the future. No rush. How would that be?"

"A man couldn't ask for more, could he?" Johnny said, but he was scowling.

"Do you want to hear the other propositions?"

"Why not?"

"Then the second is this," Rich said. "The situation in and around Georgia City has been getting worse. That is, it's getting worse for the small ranchers. Ben Mohegan squats in the middle of the valley, and he's getting more powerful all the time. About a month ago he closed all roads over his land. That means that the ranchers on Crows' Bench, and off to the west on Ute Flats, have to go miles out of their way to get to town. That's only one of his nasty tricks. Howie Fry, Waddington, Buell, Haspwell, and a few of the other small ranchers are ready to fight back, but they need a leader. And they need someone to show them how to fight. You can have the job. It isn't one I'd want. Ben Mohegan has got a new foreman named Dal Osborne. He's not much more than a gunslinger. And he's hired others of the same type—a man named Slim Donovan—another called Kelso—another known as Shadow Wells. I could list a few more. How does it sound?"

"It doesn't interest me worth a damn."

"You used to have a stake in Georgia Valley."

"When I lived here, and when my folks were here. But my parents died while I was in prison, and their land was sold. It didn't pay more than the debts that were owed. So I have no more interest in what happened here. I hope Ben Mohegan gets smashed—but someone else can do the job. You said there was a third proposition."

"Yes—but I don't know what it entails."

"A blind proposition?"

"Blind to me."

"Let's have it."

"Edith Brooks wants to see you."

"Edith Brooks? Who's she?"

"Edith Brooks is—Edith Brooks. In other words, I don't know much about her. She came to Georgia City about three months ago and opened a dressmaking shop. It's a new venture. She hasn't had much business, but maybe she doesn't need to make much money. She's got over ten thousand dollars in the bank—but that's a secret. It's not generally known."

Johnny whistled. "Keep on talking."

"There's not much more I can tell you. If I had to guess I would say that Edith is about twenty-five. She's tall, slender, and rather attractive. She wears a wedding ring but I don't know whether her husband is living or dead. She never speaks of him—or of herself. I don't know where she's from. I don't know anything about her people. I think she's western. At least she knows about ranching and she can ride a horse like a man."

"What does she want of me?"

"I can't tell you. I can't even guess. She's an intense person. Nervous. Edgy. I think there's something in her background that might have been rather violent. I get that feeling. She's wound up tight, on the brink of an explosion. Maybe she wants you to protect her. Maybe she wants you to shoot someone. Or maybe I'm way off. I really don't know why she wants you."

"How did she learn about me?"

"Probably from Merth. They're not close, but

at least they've talked to each other a few times. Merth likes her."

"Where is she, Rich? With the posse chasing me, I'm not exactly a free agent."

"This is going to surprise you," Rich said smiling. "Last night I took her to a line shack on George Haspwell's ranch, well up in the edge of the hills. She's going to wait there until she hears from me. I told her you might not be interested."

"I don't think I am," Johnny said frowning.

"Hell—you don't know what she wants."

"I can guess, Rich, and so can you. I just got out of prison. I wear a gun—and I'm good with it. But I never want to have to use it. What happened in Georgia City was an accident, or it could be blamed on the past, or on my name. If I head up into the Oregon territory, no one will care about who I was."

"Is that where you're going?"

"I think so."

"How much money do you have?"

"Damned little."

"At least, you could talk to Edith Brooks. I don't know what she wants. Neither do you. But she might ask for something you could do—and it might pay in money."

Johnny scrubbed his jaw. His three-day beard was beginning to itch. He needed a shave. But before that he wanted about a gallon of water and something to eat. He stood up, suddenly terribly thirsty and hungry. He glanced up at the sky.

"It's going to be a black night," Rich said. "I wish we were out of the hills. With no trouble at all, I could get lost."

"We won't get lost," Johnny said. "Are you sure the posse went back to Macey's?"

"Reasonably sure."

"Then we'll head for a spring I know of, not far away. I've been out of water all day. After that, we'll find those supplies you brought, and we'll eat."

"And then—"

Johnny sighed. He was afraid he was making a mistake, but he said, "Then, we'll ride to George Haspwell's line shack. I'd like to see what Edith Brooks has to offer."

# II

As they made a campfire supper, Rich didn't have much to say. Nor did Johnny. He thought of a dozen questions he could have asked about Edith Brooks, but he let the matter go. And he was rather glad that Rich didn't bring up Merth's name. He had decided abruptly that he never wanted to see Merth again—which was rather strange. Once, he would have risked almost anything to reach her side.

It seemed to him that there were two ways at which he could look at the marriage of Rich Gilmore and Merth Haspwell. He could think of Merth as having been unfaithful to her promises, or weak, and he could believe that Rich had taken advantage of her, that he had deceived her. Or to be more practical, he could imagine they had fallen in love and were swept to the point of wanting to get married—and to hell with him. He was away in prison, out of the picture. He might never come back, or if he did, he might have changed.

He knew Merth, and he knew Rich. Certainly, Merth hadn't been a weak person. Rich, in spite of his persuasive powers, he couldn't have talked her into a marriage unless she had wanted it that way. That being the case, there wasn't a thing

Johnny could do. If Rich and Merth had wanted each other—that was that. The thing for him to do was to forget them—and as soon as possible.

"We ought to get started," he said gruffly. "I know a few shortcuts. We can stay to the hills. I doubt if we'll run into anyone—but what if we do?"

Rich shrugged. "We'll worry about that, if it happens."

"But where do you stand, Rich?"

"You mean with respect to Ben Mohegan?"

"Yes."

"I handle his legal work. I do the same for most everyone else. I haven't had to take sides."

"What if you have to?"

His answer showed a trace of irritation. "What do you care, Johnny? You're not interested in the valley. It's a long ride. Let's get started."

Johnny didn't push the matter. Actually, he couldn't. If he wasn't interested in the struggle between Mohegan and the others, he couldn't insist on knowing where Rich stood. But it was still something he could speculate about. Rich Gilmore, as he remembered him, always had been cautious about committing himself. Others could lead, he would follow. If the venture was successful, he took a quiet part in the victory. If the venture failed, he disappeared. He was never numbered among those who had to stand punishment. Possibly, the best way to characterize him would be to say that Rich Gilmore was for himself. Johnny wondered abruptly why he had ever liked him.

They took a twisting course through the hills, and a good part of the way was easy riding. The night was as dark as Rich had predicted, but only the upper reaches of the Pothole Hills were heavily wooded, and they kept away from there. Toward midnight they splashed across another creek, topped a low hump of land, then dropped down into a scattering stand of timber. They rode on through the wooded area for another quarter of a mile, then Johnny reined up. He pointed to the vague, shadowy structure to the side, and said, "Here we are, Rich. Made it right on the nose."

"Don't see how you found it," Rich answered, a grudging wonder in his voice. "I didn't know where we were."

"You seem to forget I grew up in these hills."

"So did I, but I never had a sense of direction. We'll wake up Edith."

They rode toward the line shack. Beyond it, and deeper in the trees, a tethered horse, hidden in the darkness, gave a whinnied welcome, and when they reined up nearer, the door opened slightly. Through this opening, a rifle barrel appeared, and a woman's voice called a query. "Who's there?"

"It's me, Rich Gilmore," Rich answered. "Johnny Lang is with me."

"Tie your horses and come in," Edith Brooks answered. "Give me just a minute to tidy up."

They dismounted, tied their horses, and as they waited briefly, Johnny rolled a cigaret and lit it. He scrubbed his jaw again, wishing he had taken the time to shave, but an instant later was amused at himself. What difference did it make how he looked? Without much question he wouldn't agree to whatever the woman wanted.

Inside the shack, a lantern was lighted. Then the door opened, and against the background of the dim lantern light, the woman appeared. She was tall, slender, and stiffly erect. "I am ready, now," she said.

Her hair was brown and combed tightly back against her head, emphasizing her high forehead. Her eyes were steady, direct, and her smile was only surface deep. Johnny could sense the tension she was feeling. She didn't put out her hand when Rich introduced him. Her nod was almost imperceptible. She said, "Hello, Johnny Lang." And then she turned to Rich. "I kept the stove burning. The coffee's hot."

"That's good, Edith," Rich said. "It's nippy outside."

He found some cups and walked to the stove to pour the coffee. The woman looked at Johnny, then quickly looked away. Johnny was searching her face. Perhaps he had never before met Edith Brooks, but even as he told himself that, he shook his head. Something about her was naggingly familiar. Something in her manner, or something in her face made him almost sure he had seen her before.

That didn't make sense, at all. He didn't have a wide acquaintance with women. For the five past years he had been in prison where he had seen no women at all. Before then, he had lived here in Georgia Valley. Occasionally, of course, he made trips to Bradontown, Kimberly, and Springerville. And to a few other towns, not too far away. But those trips hardly counted, and such women as he had met were very few. In view of that, if he had ever met this woman before, it almost had to be somewhere around here—and according to Rich Gilmore, she was a stranger.

They had coffee, sitting on box chairs at a plank table.

The woman leaned forward. "You can leave now, Rich. I'd really like to talk to Johnny alone."

That seemed to startle the man. He looked quickly at Johnny.

"We're both adults," the woman said smiling.

"Sure, but—"

Johnny spoke sarcastically. "Rich has just remembered that I'm an ex-convict—not to be trusted."

"No, it isn't that," Rich said quickly. "I just—"

"I'm not worried," the woman said. And then

her voice softened. “Please understand me, Rich. I know what I’m doing.”

Johnny took a sudden, deep breath. It hit him who the woman was. He nearly cried the name aloud—but didn’t. Was it possible that Rich didn’t know her true name? He looked searchingly at the woman, trying to test what he had thought, and abruptly, wasn’t sure he had been right.

“I didn’t mean it as it sounded, Johnny,” Rich was saying. “The fact you’ve been in prison makes no difference to me. Will I see you again?”

“I don’t know,” Johnny said, but he wasn’t thinking about Rich Gilmore. This woman was much more interesting.

“Good luck, anyhow,” Rich called from the door.

He stepped outside, and a moment later, Johnny heard the sound of Rich Gilmore’s horse, pounding away. Then, for perhaps half a minute, neither Johnny nor the woman, spoke.

She was the one to break the silence. “Well, Johnny?”

He looked at her boldly. “Hello, Dru.”

Her lips twitched. “When did you guess?”

“Just a moment ago—when you said you knew what you were doing. Dru Mohegan always knew exactly what she wanted of life.”

“She hasn’t done too well.”

“Neither have I. More coffee?”

"Yes, I'd like more coffee."

Johnny filled their cups. He said, "Where do we start, Dru? What's this stuff about Edith Brooks?"

"Just a name I borrowed."

"And the wedding band on your finger?"

"I bought it in a store. A woman who seems married has more status than one who is single."

"You mean you're living under that name—as Mrs. Edith Brooks."

"That's right, Johnny."

"How many know you're Dru Mohegan?"

"No one in the valley. At least, I don't think anyone knows. Don't be surprised. When I left here with my mother, I was only twelve. I've changed a great deal. When I returned, a few months ago, a grown young woman very stylishly dressed, with a wedding ring, and obviously fairly well off, why should anyone have thought I was Dru Mohegan. You wouldn't have been suspicious yourself if this wasn't a rather strange meeting."

"Merth doesn't know who you are?"

"No. Or Rich Gilmore."

"How about your father?"

She stiffened instantly and looked away. Her voice was strained as she answered. "No, he doesn't know me."

"Rich said you had ten thousand dollars in the bank."

"I do, but I didn't know he knew about it."

"As you get to know Rich better, you'll discover he knows a great deal more than shows on the surface."

"I've rather liked him," Dru said.

Johnny dismissed Rich Gilmore from his mind. He stared at Dru and then said, "Dru, do you want to tell me about it. You've come back to Georgia City under another name; you've got ten thousand dollars in the bank, but you're working as a dressmaker; and you've met Ben Mohegan, but you haven't told him that you're his daughter. Now you've sent for me, an ex-convict, fleeing from a sheriff's posse. None of it makes sense."

"I think it does, Johnny. Do you remember when mother and I left Georgia City?"

"No. I heard you had left to visit relatives. Then we learned you weren't coming back. I never knew why. I seem to remember your mother didn't like it on a ranch—that she preferred the East."

"We had little choice," Dru said, and she sounded bitter. Her face tightened. "We had little choice. Father threw us out. He gave us transportation to Philadelphia—and not an another cent. We heard from him only once more—through an attorney. A divorce suit, charging my mother with desertion."

"She could have fought it."

"She didn't want to. You never had to live with

Ben Mohegan. Mother carried scars to her grave. She had deeper scars inside."

Johnny made another cigaret, lit it, and scowled, remembering some of the things he had heard about Ben Mohegan. His father had said, once, that Ben Mohegan was the best cattleman in the country—and the meanest man who lived, harsh to the point of brutality. Johnny had one vivid recollection of his own. A rustler had been caught by some of Mohegan's men. He had been stripped, whipped until his back was bloody, and then hanged. Ben Mohegan, himself, had directed the punishment.

This line shack was quite small—a shelter for the men working the hills, used occasionally. On its walls were two windows, a door, and a corner alcove. Its furniture amounted to two bunks, a stove, a plank table, and several box chairs. Tonight the windows were blanketed, undoubtedly hung there by Dru. Off to the side was a sack of supplies.

"Mother is dead," Dru was saying. "She died last winter. Toward the end we had money, from my grandparents, but before then, we lived like charity cases. My mother's people were extremely religious. They looked on mother's divorce as a sin. They made her suffer. I'll always hate Philadelphia."

He looked at her thoughtfully. "Why did you move to Georgia City?"

"Can't you guess?"

"I don't want to."

"Then I'll tell you, Johnny. After mother died and after all the bills were paid, I was left with ten thousand dollars. I decided to spend it in Georgia City. I came here to buy something—trouble."

"You are thinking of your father?"

"Yes. I want him to suffer as we suffered. I want to pay him back for what he did. . . . You don't think much of me, do you."

Johnny shook his head. "No, I don't. It's not worth it, Dru. I could be bitter, too. I held up one of your father's men. I took his money, but not to keep it. I would have returned the money. Ben Mohegan knew it, but the judge was his man and I went to prison for five years as a bandit. Now, I could want to get even. I could go after Ben Mohegan. If I did I'd probably get shot, or if I killed him, I'd probably have to run for the rest of my life. I don't want to do that."

Dru made a restless motion with her arm. "You think as a man thinks. You think of fighting, of settling a quarrel with your guns. With a thousand dollars, or even with less, I could hire a gunslinger to kill my father. Or I could do it myself. But that isn't what I want. My father owns a little empire, here in Georgia Valley. I want to pull it down. I want to smash it. I want to see it crumble and fall to pieces. I want Ben

Mohegan to lose every cow he owns, every acre that is his. I want to see him reduced to nothing. I want to see him suffer as mother and I suffered."

"And will that make you feel better?"

"It's something I've got to do."

"No you don't, Dru."

"But I do—and I'll manage it. Do you want to know how?"

"No."

"Aren't you interested at all?"

"No."

"Would you be tempted by—five thousand dollars?"

"No."

"Do you want it all—ten thousand dollars?"

"No."

She leaned toward him. "Then I've one more offer. If you'll help me, Johnny, I'll give you the Double M, the heart of Georgia Valley, the empire that once belonged to Ben Mohegan."

Johnny shook his head. "No, Dru. Not even for that. It means fighting—killing. It's not worth it."

She turned away, her body rigid, her arms stiff at her sides, her hands clenched. "They told me Johnny Lang had courage," she said bitterly. "They told me he was afraid of nothing. They must have lied."

Johnny shrugged and was silent. Then he raised his head, listening. Outside, a horse whinnied. Possibly Dru's horse. He was frowning, now, and listening intently. The whinnying of a horse might not mean anything, but when he and Rich rode up, Dru's horse had welcomed them with a call. Some horses always acted that way. Some didn't. What he had just heard might mean someone else had ridden up.

Dru whirled toward him. She half held out her hands and her voice had softened. "I shouldn't have said that, Johnny. But listen to me, please. Let me tell you what I have in mind."

"I'd rather have you do something else," Johnny said. "Move to the other side of the table, nearer the wall. Pull a box close to the lamp and get your hand close to it. When I tell you, turn down the light. Turn it all the way so it goes out—and right afterwards, drop to the floor."

Her eyes widened in surprise. "But why, Johnny?"

"Maybe we've got visitors. They might not represent a danger to you, but I'm in a different class. I shouldn't have come here. Who knows where you are?"

"No one but Rich Gilmore."

"It might be Rich coming back—or it's someone else who just chanced by. Get around the table. Sit down, and start talking. Talk about Philadelphia."

She didn't question his order. She circled the table, sat down, reached close to the lantern, and then started talking, her eyes shifting from the door to Johnny Lang. He had stepped to the far corner and had dropped to the floor.

A full minute passed, a second, a third. Above the murmur of Dru's voice, Johnny thought he heard a footstep outside—a stealthy footstep, hesitant, cautious. The man outside might prove to be friendly, but if he was, this was a strange way to act. Normally, the man should have moved faster, and should have made more noise.

The doorknob turned, then, someone outside, pushed it forward, but just an inch. At the table, Dru must have noticed that, for her voice faltered. She looked quickly at Johnny, her hand on the lantern, ready to turn it down. But he shook his head. His lips formed the words, "Not yet."

Dru went on talking. "No, we didn't like it in Philadelphia. The winters were cold. When it didn't snow, it rained, but the rain was icy. And in the summer . . ."

The door had been pushed wider. Then, suddenly, the man outside thrust it wide open and stepped inside. He was tall and thin, his face was shadowed by his hat, and he had a gun in each hand. Someone else was just behind him, but Johnny couldn't see the second man. The one in front swept his eyes from side to side. He didn't seem at all interested in Dru, but he seemed puzzled. "Where's Johnny Lang?" he shouted. "They told us—"

"I'm over here," Johnny said. And he meant

to say more. He meant to say that the man was covered, but he didn't have the chance. The two guns the man was holding swung toward him, and as they exploded, Johnny fired back.

"Now, Dru!" he screamed at her.

He fired again as the lamp went out and he rolled to the side and fired three times through the door. He crawled to the side again, then lay waiting. The first man in the room had been falling sideways as the light went out. He now lay somewhere in the darkness, and he wasn't moving. The man in the doorway had fired several times, but where his shots had gone, Johnny wasn't sure. He thought some of them had hit the first man. And whether he had hit the man in the doorway, he didn't know. At least, the man in the doorway wasn't shooting anymore.

Johnny reloaded his gun. He let a minute pass, then he spoke in a whisper. "Dru? Are you all right?"

"I'm all right," the woman answered. "Should I light the lamp?"

"Not yet," Johnny answered. "There was another man outside. Maybe more."

"I'll close the door."

"No. I'll close it," Johnny said.

He edged around the room and slowly pushed the door shut.

There was no more shooting. He had Dru light the lantern, then knelt at the side of the man he had shot. A moment later Johnny stood up.

"Is he—badly hurt?" Dru asked.

Johnny's words were harsh. "He's dead."

A shudder ran over the woman's frame. She looked at the figure on the floor, then turned away. "I recognized him. His name was Vic Quinn. Ten days ago, I danced with him. He was a good dancer. He laughed a lot. He worked for my father, but—"

"Why the hell do you care?" Johnny said. "If you try to tear down Ben Mohegan, this is only the beginning."

She shook her head. "You didn't listen. I don't want men killed. There's another way."

"Then you don't remember your father. Any scheme you have will end with guns. Force is the only thing Ben Mohegan respects."

"There are legal tricks."

"He would laugh at them, and if the law turned against him, he would fight back, the only way he knows. He doesn't play parlor games. He never learned."

In the moment of silence which followed, Johnny heard the sound of a horse driving away. At a guess, then, the man in the doorway had made it to his horse and was riding for help. But there could still be men outside, waiting for someone to step from the shack.

"What are you going to do?" Dru asked, and she sounded tired.

Johnny didn't have a positive answer. "I don't know, Dru. Up to a moment ago, I hadn't killed anyone. The man I wounded in the bar is recovering. No warrant would be issued for that shooting. But now things have changed. I've killed a man."

"You couldn't help it. I'm sorry about what happened but I would tell anyone you fired in self-defense."

"Sure, but that doesn't help. I'm a fugitive. The man I shot was on the side of the law. That makes me a criminal."

As an immediate step, he had to get away, and he had better do it as soon as possible. The man who had left would return with others. And he still had to worry about whether or not someone was waiting outside.

"They shouldn't have come here," Dru murmured, protesting about what had happened. "No one knew I was here."

"No one but Rich Gilmore," Johnny said bleakly.

"You don't think—"

"The man who stepped in expected to find me."

"But I still don't think that Rich—there must be some other explanation."

"I don't want to think about him," Johnny said. "Turn out the lamp again. I want to step outside."

Dru turned out the lamp. She lowered her

voice. “Johnny, be careful. If anyone else gets hurt . . .”

He didn’t answer her. Turning, he headed for the door.

# III

It was black outside. Earlier, Johnny had been able to see a few stars, but now, clouds blanketed the sky. The breeze had sharpened. At any time it might start raining. He could sense it in the smell of the air.

But he scarcely thought about that. He had stepped to the side of the door and had dropped to the ground. Probing the thick shadows he searched for any sign of movement. A dozen men could have been hidden nearby, but after several minutes he risked shifting his position. Nothing happened. He moved again, creeping away from the line shack. After a time he stood up.

Johnny turned toward the trees. He found his horse, and, not far away, another. Probably Vic Quinn's, the man he had shot. Dru's was deeper in the trees, unsaddled.

Johnny walked back to the line shack. He called to Dru that it was safe outside, and that she could relight the lantern. "Pack your stuff," he suggested. "Time to leave. How's that horse of yours?"

"He's a good horse," Dru said. "A man's horse."

"Then we'll keep him," Johnny said. "Where's your saddle?"

"In the alcove."

"I'll get it later," Johnny said.

He returned to the horses, unsaddled his and Vic Quinn's, then led them to the creek running through the meadow. There, he set the two horses free, and cut them with a whip to start them running down stream. They wouldn't run very far, but they might keep drifting down as far as Crows' Bench, and from there, might keep moving. Some of the men who came here, looking for him, might follow them.

Johnny put his own saddle on Dru's horse.

"We're taking just one horse?" Dru said, surprised.

Johnny grinned and nodded. "Just one horse. We'll have to ride double. But this isn't for any romantic reason. It's practical. The trail I'm taking won't be easy to follow."

"Where are we going?"

"To Sam Wylie's."

"Does this mean anything. I mean, since you're not leaving."

"If you're asking if I've changed my mind—I haven't. I want to get you where you're safe. What I'll do later I haven't decided, but I want no part in the struggle for the valley."

She spoke reflectively. "Sometimes, people can't help what happens."

That gave Johnny a topic to think about as they rode up the narrow meadow. Without much question, he wasn't in an enviable position. The man he had shot in Georgia City several days before would recover. He could be charged with shooting him, but since he would live, nothing much could be done to him. Tonight's experience, however, was another matter. A man searching for him had been killed. For a time, at least, he had to stay here in an attempt to clear up his record.

As the hills came together, Johnny turned to a stream. He followed it, and turned with it to the south. Where the stream twisted east Johnny left it, pressing now through a choked ravine. "You'll have to keep close to me, Dru," he told her. "Keep your head against my back or you'll get scratched by the branches."

The next hour's trip wasn't easy. The tangled growth scraped at their clothing. At several places the path was so difficult that they dismounted and walked, leading the horse. Finally, however, the underbrush thinned and they came out in the open. They stopped then for a time. Off to the east, the sky showed a faint grey. In another hour it would start growing light.

"You shouldn't be wasting this opportunity," Johnny said. "You could be arguing with me."

She didn't raise her head. "Would it do any good?"

"No."

"Then, why spend the energy. I need someone

to help me—a man—for there are some jobs a woman can't handle. If I can't get you, I'll have to look for someone else."

"Got anyone in mind?"

"Not yet. I need someone I can trust, and someone bold enough to take a few chances, but smart enough to back away from violence. I don't want more of what happened tonight. I told you Vic Quinn was a good dancer and that he had a hearty laugh. That's true. It's also true he wasn't a very fine man. He was rough, brutal. He hired out to my father as a gunslinger. Maybe it isn't a great loss to the world that he was killed, but I don't like the fact that I had something to do with it."

Johnny stared at her thoughtfully. It was too dark to see her face clearly, but from her voice he could sense she was worried. He took a deep pull at his cigaret and then said, "Dru, how honest can you be with yourself?"

She made a negative motion. "How do I know? I try to be honest with myself. Maybe I don't always succeed."

"I've just spent five years in prison," Johnny said. "I have said that those years were wasted, but I'm not sure that's true. At least, I learned a number of things while I was behind bars. I got to know a few men who were boastfully unlawful. I talked to them. Some of the tricks I learned from them may help me in the days ahead. But I learned something else from an old man who has been in prison fifteen years, and who never will leave. In fact, he doesn't have long to live. I talked to him more than anyone else. He made me think. He made me take a good look at myself."

"Do you think I haven't done that?"

"I don't know."

"You're thinking of why I'm here."

"Can't help it, Dru. I can't help asking if it's worth it. You've got ten thousand dollars. That's a good nest egg. You want to throw it away."

"It's just money, Johnny."

He took another deep pull at his cigaret. "No. You're wrong. Money laying in a bank is just money. But if you use it to water an arid land, money is something which gives life. If you use the money to pull a man down, you've bought death and sorrow."

She suddenly sounded angry. "You're talking like a preacher."

"No, I'm just trying to be honest."

"Didn't you ever hate a man?"

"Sure I have—and I will in the future. I'll try to justify my hate, but if I look at it honestly, I'll see it as destructive, and ugly, and it makes me less of a man. That's too bad, too. Do you know what old Dad Zeigler said of mankind. He's the one I mentioned in prison. He said that mankind was so mean and little and insignificant that when we pulled it lower, we were doing a risky thing. At best, we're not much better than animals."

"I don't think I'd like your Dad Zeigler. I certainly can't agree with him."

"Think about it at least. How do animals behave? . . . Time to ride on, Dru."

It started raining just after dawn, and by the time Johnny and Dru pulled up at Sam Wylie's, both were soaked. Wylie, still at home, probably because of the rain, heard them ride up, and came out on the porch. Two men working for him, busy at some task in the barn, also showed up to stare at Sam's visitors.

"Morning, folks," Wylie called uncertainly. "I reckon—" He broke off. His cyes widened and he shouted, "Johnny! Johnny Lang! Well, I'll be damned. Come right in. The lady, too."

"Aren't you worried about the posse?" Johnny asked.

"Not unless you are." He raised his voice, turning to the door. "Hey, Lucy! Look who's here."

Sam Wylie was big, thick-bodied, nearly fat, and the woman who now appeared at the door, was of comparable size. She had soft gray hair, and a round, ruddy face.

She called, "Hello, Johnny. We were afraid we'd miss you. And Mrs. Brooks, you are welcome too. Don't sit out there in rain. Sam, call to the men to take their horses."

Wylie beckoned to the two men in the barn doorway to come forward. Then he glanced at

Johnny. "How about it? Want to keep your horse handy?"

"Might as well," Johnny answered.

He dismounted, helped Dru to the ground, then turned the horses over to the two men.

Johnny and Dru went inside and were provided with dry clothing.

After they had eaten breakfast, and while they were having more coffee, Johnny explained what had happened.

Wylie's face looked thoughtful. "At least, don't be sorry about Quinn. If he's dead it means only that Ben Mohegan has one less gunslinger to throw at us when the fight starts."

"It means more than that to me," Johnny said. "It could brand me as an outlaw."

"Quinn's death could never brand you as an outlaw. He was an outlaw himself."

"If that's true, it might help. But the sheriff here—"

"We need a new sheriff," Wylie said. "In fact, we need a complete new deal: an honest judge and a fair voice for everyone in the valley. I'm glad you're back, Johnny. We need you."

Dru smiled, but she didn't speak.

Johnny didn't look at her. He shook his head definitely. "Don't be foolish. I'm not taking a hand."

"You didn't used to feel that way," Wylie said.

"Things were different five years ago," Johnny

explained. "In those days I had a stake in the Georgia Valley. My father owned a ranch, up here on Crows' Bench. But it's gone now, and my parents are dead. I don't own a blade of grass. If a fight is shaping up it's not my fight."

Lucy Wylie reached to cover his hand. "You grew up here, Johnny. This is your home. You belong here as surely as we do. Don't you think I'm right, Mrs. Brooks."

"Certainly, I think you're right," Dru said.

"Let me tell you what's been happening," Wylie said, pressing what he thought was a slight advantage. "Ben Mohegan has been spreading out until he owns nearly all of the floor of the valley. For years now, we've been going to town, following roads which crossed his land. But a few weeks ago, he closed those roads. If we want to go to town, we have to circle south to hit the old stage road. It takes Macey two days to get to town, two days back. It takes me a day and a half. The same is true of the ranches on Ute Flats, off to the west."

"What else?" Johnny shrugged. "You might as well tell me the rest."

"It would take the rest of the morning," Wylie said. "But here are a few more problems we have to deal with. Whether we like it or not, we're supposed to belong to the Georgia Valley Association. All cattle sales have to be approved by the association. Ben Mohegan runs the association."

"You don't have to work through it."

"Vern Waddington didn't. He started a herd to Springerville. It didn't get there. The herd was rustled. Two of his trail hands were killed. The sheriff here said it happened out of his territory. The sheriff in Springerville was sorry about what happened, but he had his own problems. Nothing was done."

"Keep talking."

"Bank loans have been tightened. None of us can manage any more loans—or extensions. The county board, dominated by Ben Mohegan, assessed more taxes to build a new schoolhouse and a courthouse. Mohegan got the bid to do the jobs and got the money, but hasn't done anything about it. Taxes were hiked again to give the sheriff three deputies. They've been hired and have been assigned to patrol the borders of Mohegan's land. That's a slap at us."

"What's Ben Mohegan after," Johnny asked.

Sam Wylie shook his head. "Damned if I know. Mohegan's got all the land he needs—all the water he can use. He's got all the cash money he could want. He's got a new wife, young and good looking. He's wagoned new furniture and they say it's really something. His ranch house, inside, looks like a palace. You'd think that a man with all that would lean back and take it easy—but not Mohegan. You know what I think—I think he's got a mean streak that he can't help."

Johnny got to his feet. He walked to the window and stood looking out at the rain. It was coming down steadily. In all probability, he was safe for the day. In this kind of weather the posse couldn't have trailed him very far.

Wylie came up behind him. He said, "Johnny, we're not going to take it. We're going to fight. We're going to sell our cattle where we wish. We're going to town over the old roads. We're going to challenge the right to have the sheriff hire three deputies, and assign them to ride Mohegan's borders. We're going to demand an accounting of the building funds for the schoolhouse and courthouse. But we need help. We need you."

"You mean you need my guns," Johnny said harshly.

"If it comes to that, yes. But we need more than that. We need your courage. We need your leadership. You never backed up an inch to Ben Mohegan."

"He sent me to jail."

"He owned the judge—but you didn't crawl, even then."

Johnny swung around. "How many of you are in it?"

"All of us along the bench. Every man on the flats across the valley, and some of the men in town. Our ranch hands, too. I've got a couple myself."

"They won't all stick with you."

"Most of them will."

Johnny walked back to the table. He looked at Dru, at Mrs. Wylie, and then at Wylie. They were watching him anxiously, waiting to hear what he was going to say, and he knew they wouldn't understand him. They would look on him almost as though he was a traitor. This matter of Ben Mohegan was a vital problem to them. Because he once had lived here, it should also be to him. Or at least, that's what they would think.

Shaking his head, he sat down. "I can't do it, Sam. Sure, you've got a problem on your hands—but it's not mine. And I'm not your answer."

"You could help, Johnny."

"Anyone with a gun can help. That's what you're up against. A fight. A bitter, ugly fight. It's going to cost lives. I want no part of it."

Wylie twisted his hands together. "It means nothing to you that Mohegan sent a posse after you—and with no real cause."

"I didn't like it."

"What if they brand you as a murderer because of the death of Vic Quinn?"

"I mean to clear that up," Johnny said. "I may see the sheriff, Henry Ash. If I have to, I'll see Ben Mohegan."

"How?"

"Haven't figured it out yet."

"So at least, you won't be riding away?"

"Not right away."

Wylie squinted across the room. He nearly smiled. "You'll be in it, Johnny. You won't get anywhere with the sheriff. You'll have to see Mohegan—and if you try that, you'll be up to your neck."

There was no point in arguing. Dru and Mrs. Wylie started cleaning up the table. Johnny and Sam Wylie went into the parlor.

"I suppose Mrs. Brooks would like to get back to town," Wylie suggested.

"I think she would," Johnny agreed.

"I can ride her in this afternoon, if the rain slackens. What will you do?"

"Ride in myself, but not until after dark. I'll have a talk with Henry Ash."

"Grab a coat," Wylie said. "I want to check what Chuck and Tom are doing, and it might not be a bad idea to be sure your horse is in shape—just in case you have to run."

They went outside, hurried through the rain, and entered the barn. Only one of Wylie's men was in sight. He was sitting on a box, mending a harness. When Wylie and Johnny came in, he glanced up, then looked away and kept busy.

"Chuck, where's Tom?" Wylie asked.

"Went to the bunkhouse, I reckon," Chuck answered.

Wylie stepped back to the door. He shouted, "Tom! Hey, Tom, I want to see you a minute."

He got no answer. Wylie shouted again, and stood looking outside, awaiting some reply.

To Johnny Lang, the man mending the harness seemed nervous. He was wearing his holster, and that was strange. He hadn't been wearing it earlier in the morning. And not far from where he was sitting was his rifle. The man stabbed a look at Johnny, then quickly turned away. He was a rather chunky man with a heavy jaw, and he hadn't shaved. He had a shock of iron gray hair.

Wylie swung around. He sounded angry. "All right, Chuck, let's have it. Tom didn't answer. One of the horses is gone from the corral. A saddle's gone from the rack, too. Where did Tom go?"

Chuck shrugged, but his body was tense. "How should I know where he's gone? Ain't none of my business."

Wylie walked forward, shaking his head. "You're close enough, you and Tom. Don't give me that stuff. Where did he go?"

Chuck jerked to his feet. Perhaps it was an accident, but he stepped to where the rifle was leaning. His answer was defiant. "Damnit, I don't know. Quit riding me, Wylie."

A man usually didn't wear a gun around the place. Wylie was unarmed, but that didn't seem to worry him. "That's enough from you," he shouted hoarsely. "Pack your gear. I'll have your wages ready in five minutes."

Chuck gnawed his lips. He was suddenly perspiring. He stabbed another look at Johnny, his eyes at Johnny's middle. Under the bulky coat, he couldn't be sure whether or not Johnny was armed.

"Get a move on," Wylie snapped.

"Sure, boss. Sure," Chuck said.

He stooped over and picked up the rifle. Then he quickly leveled it and waved it from side to side, covering both Wylie and Johnny. His face had a frightened, desperate expression. His words were shaky—too high. "Stay where you are—both of you. Don't move."

Sam Wylie seemed startled. "What the hell's the idea? Damnit Chuck, put down that rifle."

"I'll not put it down," Chuck answered. "You stay right where you are 'til Tom gets back."

Johnny nodded and stepped forward. "Don't you get it, Sam? This has nothing to do with you. Tom's gone to town to get the sheriff. It could be Mohegan's posted a reward."

"Five hundred dollars," Chuck said. "More money than we'll ever get by wages."

Sam Wylie's face darkened, and as he realized what Chuck was saying, his anger made him shaky. He leveled his arm at Chuck and started cursing him. Then, seemingly unaware of the rifle, he lunged forward, his hands outstretched to grab him.

It was a reckless, senseless thing to do. Chuck

had been swinging the rifle to cover both men, but as Wylie dived toward him, Chuck had to whip the rifle to cover him. He fired it, and as Wylie dropped, Chuck tried to switch his aim to Johnny. He was too late, and an instant before Johnny's bullet hit him, he realized he wouldn't make it.

Reeling backwards, Chuck dropped the rifle. He turned half around, then fell on his face. He tried, once, to get up, but he couldn't raise himself.

Johnny Lang, however, scarcely noticed what happened to Chuck. He hurried to where Wylie had fallen. He had been hit through the upper arm. His sudden lunge had forced Chuck to fire quickly—and too high. The bullet only had scraped the bone. It was shock, more than anything, that had knocked Wylie down.

"You're lucky as they come," Johnny said.

He stood up and glanced at Chuck's figure. The man wasn't moving. At least, for the moment, Johnny didn't have to worry about him. He turned to the door to call Mrs. Wylie, but that wasn't necessary. Mrs. Wylie and Dru were both hurrying to the barn.

# IV

Sam Wylie was carried into the house and put to bed. Mrs. Wylie, assisted by Dru, bathed and bandaged his arm.

Johnny escaped from the bedroom. Out on the porch he had a cigaret. He wasn't exactly shaky, but he knew he wasn't far from it. He was wound up tight. His mouth was too dry. He knew that in view of Sam Wylie's testimony, no one could blame him for Chuck's death—but that didn't make him feel any better.

Dru came out. She looked at him, her eyes grave, steady, her expression immobile. She looked ridiculous in Mrs. Wylie's tent-like dress, but he didn't smile.

"If you will saddle a horse for me, I'll go for the doctor," she told him. "Mr. Wylie says it isn't necessary, but I think a doctor should look at his wound."

"I should go for the doctor," Johnny said. "But if I ran into the posse, I'd never make it."

"What are you going to do, Johnny?"

"What I said earlier. I want to talk to Henry Ashe. If I can't get satisfaction from him, I'll talk to your father."

"He'll kill you, Johnny—or one of his men will."

"Maybe not."

She showed a flash of irritation. “Surely they will—and it’s such a waste. You might just as well be in the fight.”

“My fight, Dru. I’ll fight my own fight, if I must.”

“But you won’t help your friends.”

“Friends? They want to use me, Dru. That’s what you want.”

She spoke slowly. “No, you’ve never listened to what I want. A fight is shaping up in the valley, a fight against my father. I know about that, but I’m not a part of it. I don’t intend to be a part. But I’ll take advantage of it. I must. That’s sensible. My attack on my father, however, is different. I want to hit him where it will hurt. In his pocket—and in his pride.”

He grinned at her. “I’m glad you don’t hate me.”

“Don’t you want to listen?”

“No.”

“Then will you do one thing for me? If you decide to see my father, see me first.”

“That might not be possible.”

“If you go to see the sheriff, I’m just up the street—in the building beyond the barber shop.”

Johnny planned aloud. “If Tom went for the sheriff, no matter how fast they ride, I doubt if they can get here before dark. It’ll probably be after midnight before the men get back to Georgia City. That would be a good time to see Henry Ashe—late at night, and after a tiring ride.

If I don't get what I want, I'm going directly to Ben Mohegan. But I won't try that until the next night."

"You'll have to hide somewhere. I have a cellar," Dru said.

"Large enough for my horse?" Johnny asked, grinning.

"I have a shed which would hold several horses. No one would look there."

"You're too trusting."

"But I do want to talk to you before you see my father."

Johnny evaded a direct answer. "I'll think about it, Dru. But I'm afraid we'd just argue. I'm tired of argument. I'll go saddle your horse."

"Don't forget—we have an appointment in Georgia City," Dru said as she mounted.

"Make it if I can," Johnny answered.

He watched her ride away, a tall, slender young woman. She might have been beautiful, but she wasn't. The bitterness destroying her made her cold and tense. Since meeting her he had hardly been able to think of her as a woman. On their ride here, as she sat behind him, he had been able to feel the softness of her body. But when she spoke her words reminded him of why she was here. Only in her flesh was she soft.

By mid-afternoon, Sam Wylie had only a slight fever. He wasn't worried about his wound, and anyhow, the doctor Dru had gone for would arrive sometime in the evening. Before then, undoubtedly, the posse would show up, and well ahead of them, Johnny Lang would have left.

Wylie urged him to go. "I can face the posse," he said. "Lucy's got a sharp tongue herself. Don't worry about us and don't worry about Chuck's death. No one's going to blame you for that."

"You'll want to fire the man who went after the posse," Johnny guessed. "That means you won't have any help—and you're laid up."

"I'll pick up someone. . . . For that matter, how about you?"

"I'm still in hiding."

"But that might be cleared up . . . Damnit, I want to keep you in the valley."

"Mohegan doesn't."

"Hell with Mohegan. We're going to smash him."

"You're going to smash no one, for several days at least," Johnny said grinning. "Stay in bed where you belong. I may be seeing you. Can I borrow a horse?"

"Take any one you want," Wylie offered.

An hour later, Johnny reached the sloping edge of the bench. Just below him, now, he could see the heart of the valley—Mohegan's land. Circling to the north and protected by the Pothole Hills was the area known as Crows' Bench. Off to the west, across the valley, was another wide mesa which was called Ute Flats. On Ute Flats and on Crows' Bench, half circling Ben Mohegan's land, were possibly a dozen ranches. A number were substantial spreads; a few were quite small. Taken together, they more than equalled Mohegan, but they were still divided—divided by leadership and divided by distance. Wylie had said they were united against Ben Mohegan—but he rather doubted that. Some on the bench didn't like each other, and between the bench and the flats, there had always been a sharp rivalry.

The rain didn't stop, and after it grew dark, it got cold.

It was near ten o'clock when Johnny reined up at the edge of Georgia City. The rain and the darkness made it impossible to see much of the town, but he remembered it well from the past and he had seen it, briefly, several days before. The glimpse he had had of it hadn't indicated many changes. At the far end of the main street was a livery stable where he could find shelter. It didn't used to be kept locked. It probably wasn't now. In the old days, it hadn't been attended overnight.

Johnny rode on, traveling the full length of the main street. The two saloons caught his attention, for they were still open, and showed lights inside. Excepting those, however, and the hotel, every other business building was dark. And no one was on the street.

Johnny reined up in the livery stable yard, went inside, and bedded down his horse.

It was now just after ten. If a posse had gone to Wylie's and was returning, he couldn't expect them before midnight. As things stood now he had several hours to waste.

Warm food was an interesting thought. The restaurant was closed, but he could go to Dru's, and she probably would welcome him. That meant an argument, however. Or he could try something else. During his brief, uneasy talk with Rich Gilmore here in Georgia City, Rich had said, *"Why don't you come to supper some night. Merth would like to see you, I know. We live in the Old Deering house."*

Maybe it was foolish to see Merth again. But if he could see her in Rich Gilmore's home and could see she was happy, it might be easier to forget her.

Still not sure what he would do, Johnny left the stable, then angled through the town to the Old Deering house. It had been repainted white. It glistened dully through the darkness. And someone was up, inside. He could see lights at the edges of the curtained windows.

Johnny walked up to the door, knocked, and stood waiting. He heard no voices inside, but suddenly the door opened, and Rich looked out at him. He was in his shirt sleeves and, without his hat, Johnny could see his hair was getting thin. His stomach bulged, too. When he was wearing a coat, his paunch hadn't been noticeable.

"You, Johnny!" Rich gasped, and he tried to peer past Johnny into the darkness.

"No one behind me," Johnny said.

Rich pulled him inside and closed the door. "Henry Ashe led a posse out to Wylie's this afternoon. He got word you were there."

"Stopped there for breakfast," Johnny admitted.

Rich backed away. "What happened at the line shack?"

"We were interrupted. Two men sneaked up and broke in with their guns in their hands. One got away."

"The one who was killed, Vic Quinn, worked for Ben Mohegan. The one who got away, Miller Hughes, was wounded. Both had been deputized by Henry Ashe to capture you. Hughes says they called on you to surrender. You agreed to give up, then in a surprise move you drew your gun. The sheriff has listed you as a murderer."

"That's why I'm here—to talk to Henry Ashe."

"You mean it didn't happen that way."

"No. Dru—I mean—Edith Brooks can tell you what happened."

Rich shook his head. "I'm not sure that will help—and I'm not sure it's wise. If Edith Brooks angers a man like Mohegan—well, she's a woman, and she lives alone. I wouldn't want to be in her shoes. Maybe we can think of something else."

While he was talking, someone appeared in one of the room's side doors. But it was in the shadow, and the person standing there didn't immediately move forward. It was Merth, of course. Without looking that way, Johnny could sense her presence. She was studying him. For a moment, Johnny was conscious of his appearance. He had taken off his slicker, and in his borrowed clothing from Sam Wylie, he knew he didn't look his best. But at least, he had shaved.

Merth spoke suddenly. "Hello, Johnny. I was afraid I might not see you."

She came forward as he swung toward her, and she didn't look exactly as he had expected. That puzzled him. Her features were as he remembered. Her hair, her smile, her dark clear eyes, the slender shape of her body and the grace of movement were almost exactly as he remembered but in spite of that she seemed like a stranger. She put out her hand. Johnny took it briefly. He tried to make his voice sound casual. " 'Evening, Merth. I'm afraid this is rather late for a visit."

"If you've been riding, you'd—like some coffee," she said and smiled. "Or maybe even some food."

"That would be good," Johnny nodded.

"I'll see what's in the kitchen," she said. "But

why don't we all go there. I don't want to miss any of the talk."

She seemed perfectly at ease, and her relationship with Rich must have been good for when she joined them, she touched his arm and squeezed it.

Rich, however, wasn't at ease. He asked, "Johnny, where did you leave your horse? If he's outside—"

"He's in the livery stable," Johnny said. "No one knows I'm here. And I won't stay long."

"But you can," Merth said quickly. "We have an extra room. And at least, I'm not afraid of Ben Mohegan."

That was a natural statement. Johnny couldn't help grinning.

They went to the kitchen, and it didn't take Merth very long to warm up some food. But the relationship between them was strained. Perhaps it was inherent in the situation, that it couldn't have been anything else.

"What are you going to do?" Merth asked finally.

"I'll probably head toward Oregon when I get things straightened up here," Johnny answered.

"Does that mean you're helping the men fighting Ben Mohegan?" Rich asked.

Johnny shook his head definitely.

"Then, what about Edith Brooks' proposition?"

"We couldn't reach an agreement," Johnny said.

Rich twisted his hands together. "That woman's in trouble. I don't know what it's all about. She's never told me. And I can't ask you to betray her confidence, but I feel worried about her. I'd like to help her—if I knew how."

"I'd like to help her, too," Merth said. "I have the strangest feeling I know her. That's crazy, I know."

Johnny didn't want to talk about Dru. He didn't want to worry about her. What would happen to her, or how far her bitterness toward her father would take her, he couldn't guess.

"I've another worry," he said slowly. "Rich, what did you do the other night after you left the line shack?"

"Why, I went straight home," Rich said. "I felt sort off dismissed."

"I couldn't help wondering," Johnny said. "The woman I met said only she, you and Merth, knew of the meeting. But the men who broke in expected to find me. They knew I was there."

Rich had stiffened. His face was flushed. "You think I told someone? Why would I do that? If I had wanted to do that, it would have been simpler to point out the cave where you were hiding."

"Sure," Johnny nodded. "I thought of that. But someone knew I would be in the line shack. Who could it have been?"

Rich gnawed his lips, but after a moment his eyes narrowed. "Someone could have been watching. I told you I didn't know the hills. I knew Merth's father had a line shack, but I didn't remember. I asked one of his men to give me direction—Lin Rawles."

"Lin Rawles," Merth said quickly. "You never should have trusted Lin. I've seen him with Dal Osborne, Ben Mohegan's foreman. Why didn't you ask me the way to the line shack?"

"You weren't home that day," Rich reminded her. "You were visiting south of town."

Johnny shrugged. Possibly, Lin Rawles had been curious, had talked to Dal Osborne, and a watch might have been posted at the line shack. But the matter wasn't really important. He said, "Forget it, Merth—Rich. But if you're against Ben Mohegan, maybe you ought to talk to Haspwell—warn him about Lin Rawles."

"I'll do that, next time I see him," Merth said. "I know which side I'm on. Rich hasn't decided yet, but when he gets pushed a little further, he'll go with me."

"I'm half there already," Rich said easily.

They talked for a while longer, but well before midnight, Johnny left. Then, standing outside in the darkness and ignoring the rain, he watched the house. Definitely, the two men who had jumped him in the line shack had expected him. Lin Rawles might have been responsible, but in spite of what Rich had said, it was more reasonable to blame him. Tonight, Rich knew he meant to see the sheriff. It would be interesting to see whether Rich left the house.

The minutes dragged. Johnny had found a tree to stand under, but the tree didn't keep off much of the rain. And it kept off none of the cold. After a long time, the lights in the house went off, but Johnny stayed where he was. After a while he was glad he had. *Rich was leaving the house. He came silently around the building from the rear, then turned toward the main part of town.*

Johnny followed him, then raised his head, listening. Through the rain and the wind, he heard a number of horses pounding into town—the returning posse. Rich must have heard the same sounds. He started walking faster.

Now, Johnny had to hurry. He caught up with Rich, still short of the main street. He was as silent as he could be, and in all probability, Rich had no warning of what was coming. Johnny used the barrel of his gun. He slammed it down on Rich Gilmore's head. The hat Rich was wearing broke part of the force of the blow, but he still dropped to the ground without making a cry.

Johnny knelt beside him briefly. It occurred to him that Rich Gilmore's errand to town might have been innocent, but he couldn't take a chance on that. He listened to the man's breathing, then straightened up and walked on.

# V

One of the saloons, Jourdan's, was still open, and apparently the sheriff's posse had stopped there. Eight or nine saddle horses were at the tie-rail. From the bank corner, Johnny stared that way uneasily. He hadn't considered the possibility of a stop at the saloon. Wet and cold and tired, he had thought the posse would disband, and head for shelter, each man going his own way. If that had happened, he might be able to approach the sheriff. What he should anticipate now, he didn't know.

He moved along the dark street to a point across from Jourdan's, then stood waiting. Four men came out, mounted their horses, and headed out of town to the north. From the direction they took they might have been on the way to Mohegan's. Another man left the saloon, mounted his horse, then swung around the feed store. He probably lived in town and was on his way home. But where was Henry Ashe? How long would he stay in the saloon? And what about Rich Gilmore? At any moment, Rich might recover consciousness and show up on the street.

After what seemed like a long time, two more men left the saloon. One was tall, thin, stooped—Henry Ashe. The other man was shorter, heavier.

Who he was Johnny didn't know, or care. He watched anxiously as they stopped briefly to talk. Then they separated, the short man leading two horses in the direction of the livery stable, Henry Ashe cutting across the street toward his office.

Johnny wheeled that way himself, loosening his slicker to be able to reach his gun. He called, "Sheriff, want to see you for a minute."

Ashe swung toward. "Yeah? What is it?"

"I thought we ought to have a talk," Johnny said.

He was quite close to the sheriff by this time, but the rain and the darkness hid his face. Momentarily, Ashe didn't guess who he was, and he didn't seem alarmed. Then something must have made him suspicious and he straightened a little, stiffening. He started to brush back his slicker.

"Don't try it, Ashe," Johnny said sharply. "I'm holding my gun. I don't want to use it, but if I have to, I will."

"Johnny Lang!" the sheriff gasped.

"We'll walk around the corner of the building," Johnny ordered. "It'll be a mistake if you try to start anything."

The first moment of shock was over. Ashe showed a flash of courage. "By God, no! I got twenty men across the street. All I got to do is yell. In the name of the law—"

Johnny stepped closer. "Stop it, Ashe. You don't

have twenty men across the street—and if you did, not one could get here in time to save you. Now, how about it? All I want is a few minutes of your time. Let's move around the corner of the building. *Let's do it now.*"

The sheriff took a quick look up and down the street. No one was in sight. A few men were still in the saloon, but they weren't where he could easily reach them. The gun in Johnny's hand was a substantial argument. The sheriff's body sagged. He made a weak, face-saving threat. "You'll never get away with it, Lang. Never."

"I don't want to get away with anything," Johnny said. "Just a talk. We'll go around the corner of the building."

They moved that way, off the street, and in the deep shadows they stopped.

"Now, we'll talk," Johnny said. "Don't you think it's time to admit that Will Mohegan will get well, and that he's the one who started the fight?"

This, apparently, was an argument Ashe didn't care for. "Don't know about that. But how about Vic Quinn. By God, that's something we can't forget."

"But I think you can," Johnny said. "I'll make you a proposition. Drop the charges against me, and I'll leave the valley. Will Mohegan forced the fight, but he wasn't badly hurt. Vic Quinn is dead, I know, but so far as I'm concerned, it was a matter of self-defense—just as in the case of the man I shot at Wylie's."

Ashe shook his head. "I ain't finished my investigation of that. I ain't sure Sam Wylie was telling the truth."

"Is that Ben Mohegan talking—or you?"

"By God, I'm my own man. Nobody tells me what to do."

"Then try it once. Why did you chase me after I shot Will Mohegan? You know how the fight started. You saw Will Mohegan's wound before he was taken out to the ranch. You know it wasn't bad. You had no excuse to head a posse after me. Excepting for that, I would have been out of the valley—and no trouble to anyone."

Ashe was silent for a moment, then he spoke again showing a change in attitude. "A man's got to do what he's got to do. I didn't see the shooting in the saloon. I heard Will Mohegan started it—then I got a different story. I didn't figure Will was bad hurt, then it seemed he was. So I had to pick you up. I never had nothing against you, Lang, but a sheriff's got to do his job. Then you shot Vic Quinn—"

"A gunslinger—an outlaw."

"Who said that?"

"Haven't you got a poster on him. Take a good look."

"You mean, you want to pull out—leave the valley."

"That's it exactly, but I want no charges to follow me."

"I got to think about it."

"You mean you want to ask Ben Mohegan."

"No, by God. It's just—all right, I'll make my decision now. I'll get hell for it, but be out of the valley by morning and I'll forget about you."

This was what Johnny wanted: the freedom to leave, and with no strings attached to the past. But in spite of what Henry Ashe had said, he didn't experience the relief he had expected, and that puzzled him. It hit him suddenly that Ashe might not have meant what he had said. He needed to know the truth now.

"You better get moving, if you're going to be out of the valley by morning," Ashe said. "Where's your horse?"

"In Rich Gilmore's barn, behind the Old Deering house."

"How come you left your horse there. Are you and Rich—"

"Rich didn't know anything about it," Johnny said. "Had to leave my horse somewhere, and I remembered that barn. Won't take me long to get it. Have to saddle it. After I got in I rubbed the horse down. In this kind of weather, you've got to look after your horse."

The sheriff's voice was brusk. "If I was you, I wouldn't waste any time. I'm making a hell of a concession, anyhow."

"And I appreciate it," Johnny said. "Many thanks, Ashe. You won't see me again."

He whirled away in a half-run in the direction of the Old Deering house, but he didn't go very far. Stopping, he retraced his steps. Ashe was already back across the street, entering the saloon. And almost immediately he showed up again, followed by five others—possibly everyone else in the saloon. They slanted for the bank corner, the closest direct route to the Old Deering house.

Johnny didn't have to wonder where they were going. In spite of what Ashe had said, he was Ben Mohegan's man. It had been a waste of time talking to him. He should have gone directly to Mohegan.

Circling back through the darkness, Johnny headed in the direction of the building next to the barber shop—Dru Mohegan's. He could find shelter there, and in the next few minutes, it would be wise to be off the streets.

The back of Dru's house was dark. Johnny hurried up to the door. He knocked and stood waiting. When there was no answer he knocked again, this time heavier. But there was still no reply.

Johnny rapped once more on the door, then, deciding Dru was sleeping, he tried the knob. The door wasn't locked. He opened it, stepped inside, and closed it. After that he called her name. "Dru! Dru, wake up. It's Johnny Lang."

That brought no response at all. Johnny risked a match, but then after a quick glance around the room, he blew it out. He was in Dru's kitchen but the windows weren't curtained, and a light was risky. Directly ahead was an open door, probably the door to her bedroom.

He tried calling her again. "Dru, it's Johnny. Wake up."

There was no sound from the bedroom. Johnny frowned, then moved up to the door and risked another match. It flared up in his cupped hands. Then Johnny blew it out, but he had stiffened, and he couldn't understand what he had seen. Dru wasn't here, or at least he didn't think she was. And the bedroom had been wrecked as though the result of a struggle. The bedcovers had been pulled to the floor. A chair had been knocked on its side. A bedstand had been overturned. A lamp, crushed to pieces, was on the carpet.

In the next twenty minutes Johnny searched the house. He was careful of using matches, afraid that someone outside might see the flickering lights. This complicated his work, but at the end of that period he could make a number of decisions. Dru wasn't here, but she had been here, for the kitchen stove was still warm. And only in the bedroom were there any signs of trouble. At a guess, then, someone or several men had come here, probably at night, and after Dru had retired to her bedroom. After a struggle, they had left, taking the woman with them.

It was reasonable to make another guess as to the identity of the man, or men, responsible for what had happened. Kidnapping wasn't an ordinary occasion. A man didn't risk it unless he had a sufficient excuse, or unless he was in a position not to be questioned. From what Johnny knew of the valley no one excepting Ben Mohegan felt far enough above the law to try such a thing. In addition to that, Mohegan had a motive to get his hands on Dru. He might have found out who she was. More likely, of course, he had sent his men after her because she had been at the line shack. Mohegan's men probably had taken her out to the Double M ranch house. There, in view of her identity, she certainly shouldn't be in danger. He didn't have to rush after her, but still, if he wanted to see her father, why the delay? Getting a horse might be a problem if the sheriff's men were looking for him. It occurred to him, however, that Dru's horse might be out in the shed. In bundling her off to Mohegan's, they might have used a wagon.

He walked out to the shed, and at least he was partially right in his guessing. Dru's horse was there. Johnny saddled him, rode outside, and almost blundered into two men who were heading for Dru's back door.

The two men saw him riding out of the shed. They shouted at him, ordered him to stop, then opened up with their guns. Wheeling around, Johnny fired back. He used up four bullets, but doubted if he hit either man. At least, they didn't stop shooting until their guns were empty.

Others were shouting as Johnny streaked out of town. Johnny headed south, as though out of the valley by the closest road, then he turned west, crossed Georgia Creek, and a few moments later circled north toward the Sandoval River. And he didn't worry at all about the trail he was leaving. In this kind of weather a man didn't leave a trail.

As Johnny headed up the valley it occurred to him that he knew less about this area than the surrounding territory. He was familiar with Crows' Bench, from one end to the other, and he had explored the Pothole Hills. He knew the Ute Flats and had hunted in the low Sandoval Mountains, beyond. When he had lived here there had been several roads crossing Mohegan's land. He had traveled those, but he couldn't say he knew the heart of the valley. From a distance, from the edge of the bench and from high points along the flats, he had scanned the wooded areas below, had traced the tree marked waterways, and could guess where the marshlands were. But to know a land, a man had to ride it.

The marshlands, for instance, weren't comparable to any of the surrounding area. From what he had heard, there were several marshlands on Mohegan's range, and one, in particular, was rather extensive. They lay along the Sandoval River, and had had to be fenced. There were sinkholes in the marshlands where cattle could have been lost in quicksand.

But it was a wonderful place for duck hunting, or at least, so he had heard. Ben Mohegan had a hunting lodge somewhere on the largest marshland, and in the spring and fall, he went there quite often.

Another thing interested him. He had never been to the Double M ranch house. He knew about where it was. He didn't think he would have any trouble finding it, even in the darkness. Others, who had been in Ben Mohegan's home, had told him about it. From what he had heard, it was an unusual building, the exterior partially stone, partially log, the roof high and shingled, some of the windows gabled. Inside, the house was paneled with expensive wood, and the furnishings were quite costly.

Mohegan had built his house on high land above the confluence of Yukon Creek and Sandoval Creek. Timberland banked it to the north and across the yard, the river had been bridged. The bunkhouse and the corral were across the river. The barn, too. In effect, the river separated the ranch house from his business efforts. It also emphasized to his ranch hands his importance as master. His men were rarely invited to the house.

Johnny Lang, heading north across Mohegan's land, came to one of the fenced marshlands. Without the fence, and in the darkness of the night, he might have ridden into it. Following the fence he came to the Sandoval River, forded it, and climbed to the road beyond. From there on, he took the road.

Gradually, the rain slackened. In another hour, it stopped. It was near dawn and off to the east the sky was brighter. Johnny decided to approach the ranch house through the wooded area to the north. How near he could get to the main building, he didn't know, but he would find out. And if he could get near it, he would stay under cover until he could walk up to the house and barge in.

It was full morning by the time Johnny crept through the trees toward the Double M ranch house. He had left his horse deeper in the timberland, and out of sight. He kept out of sight himself—or at least, he thought he had.

At the Double M, breakfast was over. In the yard across the river, the men were saddling up. Johnny counted fourteen riders.

One of the men left the yard, heading across the bridge toward the main house. He was tall and thin, and he walked with a slouch. From where Johnny was hiding he couldn't see the details of the man's face, but he had the impression that he wasn't old. At a guess, Johnny figured the man was Dal Osborne, the foreman, reporting to Mohegan for some final instructions.

For several minutes the man disappeared and was hidden by the house. Then he came in sight, returning toward the bridge. After he had crossed it, he and most of the other men mounted up and rode away, slanting southeast in the direction of Georgia City. Five men still remained across the river. In the barn or in the bunkhouse, there might be several more.

If he was going to see Ben Mohegan alone, this was the time to do it. He might never have a better chance. Johnny shot a look at the yard across the river. The men there might see him as he approached the house, but they were too far away to block him.

Johnny stood up. He unbuttoned his slicker and reached underneath to loosen his holster gun. Then he plodded straight ahead toward the ranch house. He reached the side of the building, rounded the front corner, and climbed the porch. The porch extended the full length of the building. The steps and the front door were in the middle.

After a dozen steps and half-way to the door, Johnny stopped. Someone was coming out. A woman. And at first, Johnny thought it was Dru. Almost immediately, however, he realized he was wrong. It was a young woman who had stepped in sight—but not Dru. She was slender, tall, and fashionably dressed. She wore a long gown, bustled at the hips, tight at the waist and under the jacket, and cut quite low at the breast. Her hat was wide-brimmed and flowered, but her hair was the color of the desert sands. Dru's hair was brown.

"Sylvia!" someone inside shouted, and it probably was Ben Mohegan. "Syl! Wait a minute. At least I can walk you across the bridge."

The woman's answer was icy. "That isn't necessary. I prefer to go alone. I wish—"

Her voice choked up as she saw Johnny. She raised her hands to her throat and stared at him, her eyes wide and extended. They were a startling blue. She was beautiful, too. Her skin had a creamy look. Her lips were a vivid red.

Johnny spoke, his voice low. "Don't worry about me, ma'am, I just want to see your husband for a moment."

Johnny wasn't sure of it, but he had decided that this woman was Ben Mohegan's new wife.

She tried to speak, or at least her mouth moved, but she was too startled to get the words out.

Inside the house and nearer the door, Mohegan spoke again, and he sounded angry. "Damnit, Syl, we got to keep up appearance. I'll walk you across the bridge. I don't see why—*what's wrong with you?*"

Those last words were sharp and louder. Johnny Lang felt the heavy weight of a growing anxiety. He didn't know what Ben Mohegan would do when he saw him. He might instantly grab for his gun. Johnny had hoped to command the situation, at least for a moment, long enough to say a few things. If he and Ben Mohegan could have a talk, shooting wouldn't be necessary. But with a woman in the way . . .

That was exactly what happened. Ben Mohegan stepped outside. He stepped out directly behind the woman, and his gun was in his hand. He looked past her at Johnny, and his face was ugly.

"Mohegan," Johnny said quickly. "I'm not reaching for a gun. I want—"

That was all he got to say. Behind the protection of the woman's body, Ben Mohegan raised his gun. He took deliberate aim and fired.

Pain exploded in Johnny's head. A red film blinded his eyes. It seemed to be smothering him. He pitched backward, but he had no memory of crashing to the floor.

# VI

Johnny awoke in the barn. He was bound hand and foot, and the bandage around his skull covered one of his eyes. The pounding pain in his head made him dizzy, sick at the stomach, and at first he couldn't think. Then, gradually, he remembered what had happened up to the moment he had faced Ben Mohegan.

It wasn't hard, now, to realize that Mohegan had creased him. Then, following that, his head had been bandaged and someone had tied his hands and feet and carried him across the bridge to the barn. It was still daylight, but what hour it was he couldn't guess. And at least, here in the barn, he had been put down on a straw mattress, probably borrowed from the bunkhouse. He wondered who was responsible for that. Mohegan, he was sure, hadn't ordered the mattress. In fact, in view of what he knew about the man, it was surprising he was alive—or that his head had been bandaged.

Someone entered the barn, walked up to where he was lying, and stood looking down at him. A thin, hollow-chested man, with a face so tight-skinned that his jaw and cheek bones could be outlined. He had a hacking cough, too. The man prodded him with his boot, then said, "Too bad. Figgered on makin' five hundred dollars on you. Planned to nail you myself."

"Who are you?" Johnny asked.

"They call me Shadow Wells."

"Cut me free," Johnny said. "Maybe the reward on my head would still be good."

The man coughed, wiped his face, and then grunted. "Wish I could. No fun in stretchin' a man's neck. That's what they're savin' you for."

Someone entered the barn, walked toward them, and made a growling comment. "Can't trust anyone. As I remember it, I was to guard Johnny Lang. Everyone else was to keep out. That means you."

"I go where I damned please," Shadow snapped. "Don't gimme any orders, you goddam 'breed!"

The man joining them was old, wrinkled and brown-skinned. Johnny had forgotten about him, but he remembered now. He was known as Pache Yates. Johnny had known him from the days of his childhood. He wore a gun, but his favorite weapon was a knife. He was a wizard with it. And right now he was fingering his knife as he glared at Shadow Wells.

"Did you hear me?" Shadow said harshly. "No orders."

Pache's voice was low. "Git out, gunslinger. Git out now."

The two men backed apart, but before anything serious happened a man from the door shouted, "Hey, Shadow. Boss wants to see you."

Shadow swung toward the door. He stopped, looked back, and said, "I ain't forgettin' this, 'breed. I'll be seein' you again."

He turned again and left the barn. After he disappeared, Pache spit disgustedly, then glanced at Johnny, and said, strangely, "Sorry to see you there, Johnny Lang. Never should have come back."

"Didn't mean to stay," Johnny said. "How have you been, Pache?"

"Not too good. Been having the misery."

"Then you weren't with the posse when I was hidden in the Potholes."

"Nope. If I'd been there we'd have found you. Know the Potholes well as you do. Knew 'em long ago. My people used to live there. Went there for clay."

He was referring to the Apache tribe with whom he had been reared. His mother had been an Indian.

Johnny shifted his position. "What's Mohegan going to do with *me?*"

Pache's answer was blunt. "Hang you, most likely."

"Why?"

" 'Cause Ben can't help it."

"That's a hell of a statement."

"True."

"But I don't get it, Pache. What do you mean?"

The old man wagged his head. "Don't want to

talk about it. Nothing I can do, anyhow. Was a time Syl could have saved you, but no more."

"Mohegan's wife? What does she have to do with it?"

Pache motioned angrily with his arm. "Damnit, Johnny. I said I don't want to talk about it."

He turned away, walked back to the door, and looked out in the yard. An old man, half-Indian, never really accepted in the valley, but loyal to Ben Mohegan. And much like him some people said: bitter, cruel, sadistic. In the years Johnny had known him, he had never had trouble with him, but he knew he couldn't expect any help from him.

The burning pain in his head continued. Johnny had recovered enough to be able to think, but he still felt weak. He tested the bonds around his wrists, decided he couldn't pull free, and stopped struggling. Then, staring up at the roofed loft above him, he started wondering about the woman he had seen on the porch—Syl Mohegan.

After Dru and her mother had left the valley and after the divorce, Mohegan had married again. His second wife, as Johnny remembered her, was a tall, gaunt, unsmiling woman, with a spine as stiff as a poker. He hadn't thought of her as a pleasant person, but then he might have been conditioned about her by his opinions of her husband. Actually, she might have been a gracious person. He didn't know. He had seen her, but had never talked to her. She didn't come to town often.

Then, while he had been at prison, she must have died, or she might have left. At any rate, Mohegan had a new wife. This time a young one, and rather pretty.

Pache Yates' remark about the woman had been rather interesting. *Once, Syl Mohegan could have saved him. Now, she couldn't.* What exactly did he mean? . . .

Voices at the door caught his attention. Pache Yates was talking to someone outside, but he couldn't hear what was being said. Then the man came in and Johnny saw it was Ben Mohegan. Instinctively, Johnny's muscles tightened.

Ben Mohegan weighed well over two hundred pounds; he stood more than six feet tall. He was a big, heavy, thick-bodied man. He had a full face, with an over-sized nose, puffy cheeks, thick lips and bulging jaws. Johnny had never seen him smile. He seemed to wear an habitual scowl, his eyes hard, direct and unblinking.

The man left Pache at the door, moved toward Johnny, then stood above him, staring down. He didn't say anything for a moment, and Johnny didn't speak. He half expected Mohegan to lash out at him with his boot, but he didn't.

Finally the man spoke, and his words were characteristic. "I'm waiting to hear you start whining."

"You can go to hell," Johnny said flatly.

Mohegan grunted. "You'll whine. You'll scream like a woman when you feel the rope getting tighter around your neck."

"Where's this going to happen?"

"Who cares?" Mohegan shrugged. He started away, but then swung back again and spoke again, showing a trace of irritation. "Damnit, Lang—why did you have to come back? Ain't I got enough trouble already?"

Johnny shook his head. "I didn't bring any. Sure I shot your nephew, but he asked for it. I could have shot lower. I didn't."

Mohegan motioned with his arm, as though what he had said wasn't important. "Hell with that. I know you, Johnny Lang. You're a copy of your old man. You're a troublemaker. There's already too many kicking up their hells, fussing at me. Don't need any more."

"Do you know why I came here?"

"To kill me. That's why you're going to hang."

"I came to talk to you."

"With a gun."

"Sure I had a gun. But I came here to talk—to make a proposition."

"I don't listen to propositions. I make 'em."

"But you might have listened," Johnny said. "When I went into Jourdan's saloon in Georgia City the other day, I meant to have a drink. Then I planned to go out, climb my horse, and ride away. I was leaving the valley forever. Instead, your nephew started a fight. I still meant to leave, but you sent a posse after me and my horse got lame. I had to duck under cover."

Ben Mohegan stood scowling at him, and possibly he was weighing what he had heard. But he didn't think about it very long. He shook his head. "Starting to whine, already. What I expected. After it gets dark . . ."

He broke off what he was saying and swung to look toward the door. An altercation was going on at the entrance to the barn. Pache Yates was trying to keep someone from coming in. He wasn't successful. Syl Mohegan brushed past him, ignoring his arguments. It was light enough in the barn to see the angry flush on her cheeks.

At first, she ignored Johnny. Her eyes were on her husband, and her voice was shaky with emotion. "You tell that 'breed to keep his hands to himself. If he ever touches me again, I'll use a whip on him."

"Pache was only doing what I ordered," Mohegan muttered.

"Then give him another order," Syl said. "Tell him, never to touch me."

"I'll tell him," Mohegan said.

Johnny took a thoughtful look at Ben Mohegan—and he was surprised. He had thought of him as hard as iron and with no weak spots in his armor. But here was a woman who could whip him with her tongue and who could make him uncertain of himself. His expression had changed. His lips were working. The tight set of his face had fallen to pieces.

"What are you going to do about him?" Syl asked, pointing down at Johnny.

"We're holding him for the sheriff," Morgan said.

"Then why isn't the sheriff here? It's almost sundown."

"Must have been he was busy, Syl."

She shook her head. "I don't believe it. I heard some of the men talking—talking of a hanging."

"It was just talk."

The woman took a deep breath. "It better be just talk. I'll not stand for a hanging. If you ever do anything like that, I'll leave. You'll never see me again. I mean it, Ben. I mean every word I said."

"You don't have to worry, Syl," Mohegan said. "I wouldn't do anything to make you leave."

That should have satisfied her, but it didn't. She stared narrowly at her husband. Then she said, "Ben, I want to be here when you turn the man over to the sheriff. I want to be sure what happens."

"You can be here," Mohegan said.

He didn't like it, however. That was very apparent to Johnny. Mohegan's face was tightening up again. His hands had clenched. He had taken just about all he could. He had crawled—and he wasn't the kind of man to crawl.

The woman seemed to sense that, too. Her attitude changed. She had been caustic and shrewish, but in an instant she softened and became wholly woman. She stretched her hand toward her husband and lowered her voice. "Ben, I'm sorry—we used to be so close. I haven't been happy for a long time. Maybe . . ."

"Everything's going to be all right, Syl," Mohegan said. "You know how I feel about you."

He grabbed her hand. Johnny was sure that if he hadn't been there Mohegan would have swept the woman in his arms.

"Let's go back to the house," Syl said. "We'll have a long talk."

"Sure, just like old days," Mohegan said.

He didn't look at Johnny again. Nor did Syl. They turned and walked out of the door. Almost immediately, Pache Yates walked forward, a crooked smile on his leathery face.

"Women!" he said, and he turned his head to spit.

"I like them," Johnny said.

"Yep. One of 'em just bought you a pardon. Trouble is—it won't last. Know her too well. Wish Ben did. That Syl belongs in a bordello. That's where she'll end, if Ben doesn't kill her someday. Ben never had any luck with his woman."

"How about his first wife?"

"No spunk. Like a woman I had once. Scared of her shadow. Cried all the time. Had to get rid of her, just like Ben did."

"And his second wife?"

"She nearly nagged him to death. Never let up. Tried to run him. Ben finally chased her off. Should have been luckier with his third wife—but he wasn't. Reckon I talk too much but that won't hurt. You're a dead man, anyhow. Just a question of time."

Johnny was glad that Pache Yates had been named to guard him. In all probability no one else knew Mohegan any better, and although Pache didn't say very much, his few comments were quite revealing.

"What about the other woman here at the ranch?"

Johnny Pache squinted at him. "What other woman?"

"Edith Brooks."

"Don't know any Edith Brooks."

"Then suppose I asked about Dru Mohegan?"

"How did you know?"

"She told me herself. How did Mohegan take it?"

Pache grinned. "Don't know, exactly. Maybe Ben's half scared of her. Don't know what to do with her. Didn't figger on her."

"Where's he keeping her?"

“She’s in the house, I reckon. Told me she could go any place, ’cept she can’t leave. Can’t have a horse. Ain’t supposed to cross the bridge.”

Johnny decided that for the moment he didn’t have to worry about Dru. His own problem was more desperate. Because of Syl’s intervention he didn’t have to worry about being hanged—right away. And maybe he would be turned over to the sheriff.

But that didn’t solve his problem. Henry Ashe took his orders from Ben Mohegan. He could be turned over to the sheriff—but might never reach town. A bullet in the back was just as final as a rope around the neck. If he wanted to live, the only way to be sure of it was to escape.

It grew dark, but as the shadows in the barn began to thicken, Pache found two lanterns. He lit them, and hung them up near where Johnny was lying. After a time, they heard the supper gong.

Pache didn’t answer the call. A while later, however, a man came to relieve him. The man who took his place was wholly uncommunicative. He wouldn’t talk or answer any questions. In about twenty minutes Pache Yates returned, and the man left.

“Don’t I get anything to eat?” Johnny asked.

“No one said anything about it,” Pache answered. “Reckon Ben didn’t think it was important.”

"They even give a condemned man his supper."

"Well, you're condemned all right. But this ain't exactly like a prison. Ben Mohegan makes the rules."

# VII

The minutes piled up slowly. They added up to more than an hour. Someone rode into the yard, then a little while later, Johnny heard a confusion of sounds, and guessed that a number of the men were saddling up. Soon after that he heard horses pounding away, heading to the south.

Following that, it was quiet. Another hour slipped by. One of the lanterns low on oil, started blinking. Pache noticed it, sighed, and got up. He started to refill it, but before he could there were noises at the barndoor, and three men came in. One was Ben Mohegan. The other two—scowling, hard-faced men—Johnny didn't know.

Mohegan walked forward, swinging his arms, his hands clenched. He stared down at Johnny and it was apparent that something had stirred him up. His face was flushed. He was breathing too heavily.

"I'm glad you came to see me again," Johnny said. "We didn't finish our talk."

"The hell we didn't," Mohegan answered. "We got nothing to talk about."

"Then I do," Johnny said. "When I came back—"

He didn't get to finish. Mohegan stepped closer and lashed out with his boot. A sharp pain stabbed through Johnny's side. He couldn't smother a gasp. Mohegan used his boot again. Johnny tried to roll away from it, but it was impossible.

"Tex—Parrish," Mohegan ordered, "Get him on his feet. Lash him against that timber to the side. Strip off his coat and shirt and tie his hands above his head. Then get me my whip."

The two men stooped over Johnny, freed his hands, and peeled off his coat and shirt. Then they pulled him to his feet and began dragging him to the post.

In another moment, they would be roping him in position, his body tied erect, his hands lashed to a nail above his head. *But that was where the lantern was—the lantern still burning.* Sagging between the two men, Johnny looked at the lantern. If he could reach it, smash it, and then jerk away, he might have a chance to escape. It would be his last opportunity, too. After a few minutes punishment under Mohegan's whip, he would be too weak to try anything.

Johnny sagged between the two men dragging him toward the timber. But then as he reached it, he jerked his arms up, lunging against one of the men and knocking him off balance. He heard the other one give a warning shout, and grab at him more tightly, but by then he had reached the lantern and jerked it free. Twisting, Johnny brought the lantern down on the man's head.

The man sagged to the ground. Johnny dropped down, too. Bullets from Mohegan's gun screamed above his head, spraying from side to side. And one found a target. The man Johnny had knocked off balance had jerked erect. He might have reached toward Johnny, but he didn't make it. A hoarse cry broke from his throat, and he plowed to the ground again, knocked down by Mohegan's bullet.

Crouching down close to the earth, Johnny found the holster of the man he had hit with the lantern. His hand closed around the gun. He pulled it free, but as he did so, the man rolled toward him, recovering from the shock of the blow. A fist slashed at Johnny's face, scraping his cheek. The man struck at him again, but that was all. Johnny pressed the gun against the man's body. He squeezed the trigger, once—twice. One shot probably would have been enough.

Johnny rolled away, then lay motionless, staring in the direction where he thought Mohegan might be. The man had stopped shooting, possibly to reload his gun. Johnny thought he knew where Mohegan was—but he couldn't be sure. In the blackness of the barn he couldn't see anything. Off to the side, the man Mohegan had shot was groaning, but above those sounds, nothing could be heard. And that was puzzling. The shooting in the barn should have brought everyone here. Johnny thought for a moment, then decided that all the rest must have left with the group that took off toward the south.

Mohegan's voice came through the darkness in a hoarse whisper. "Tex—Parrish—where the hell are you?"

No one answered. Johnny peered through the darkness in the direction of the man's voice. He was scowling. The voice he had heard seemed to come from the left of where he had expected. Possibly, Mohegan had changed positions. And possibly, after what he had just said, he had changed positions again. All Johnny could do was wait. He had two men to worry about. Mohegan and Pache Yates. If he risked a shot, he wanted to be sure where he was shooting.

Mohegan spoke again, and his voice this time came from the right. "Pache, where are you?"

"Back here by the door," Pache answered.

"Hell with that," Mohegan said. "Maybe Lang's down. Find out."

"Find out yourself," Pache growled. "You started all this mess. I didn't."

"Why, God damn you."

"Keep talking—you might draw a shot," Pache warned.

The two men fell silent. Johnny sat up. He laid his gun aside and quietly untied his ankles. Then he picked up his gun and stretched out on the ground.

After a brief interval, Mohegan spoke, and he seemed to have backed off toward the door.

"Pache, I think they're all down. Mind getting a lantern?"

The old man didn't answer.

"Pache!" Mohegan said again.

Still no answer.

Mohegan sucked in an audible breath. "That does it. You're finished here, Pache. Next time I see you—"

Johnny heard a blow, then the sound of someone falling. He rolled over and sat up, straining his eyes against the darkness.

Pache spoke. "Johnny, you there somewhere?"

Johnny hesitated, then risked an answer. "Right here, Pache."

"Bad hurt?"

"No."

Pache sighed, then he spoke regretfully. "Sorry about this, but I knew it was coming someday. If I hadn't have put Ben down, he'd have shot me. He won't take any sass. I'll be pulling out afore he wakes up. If you want to grab a horse, I'll be looking the other way."

Johnny stood up. "Where are the other men?"

"Don't know. Rode somewhere in a hurry. Might be back anytime. No time to lose."

"What about Ben Mohegan?"

"I'm gonna leave him where he is. So are you. He ain't hurt bad. Might be after me. Might be after you. Maybe I ought to finish him—but I owe him too much. That's the way it is."

Johnny walked forward, but he kept his gun ready for use. He said, "All right by me, Pache. I'm not through with Mohegan, but I'll handle him in my own way."

"If you're smart, you'll ride."

Johnny nodded. He waited as Pache opened the door, then, in the gray light from the sky outside, he saw the old man move in sight, and nothing in his attitude was threatening.

"I'll borrow a horse," Johnny said, forming a tentative plan. "Who's at the main house?"

"Just the two women. Syl and Mohegan's daughter. There's a cook and two servants. Mexicans. Live in the back of the wing. But you leave the woman alone, Johnny."

"I want to talk to Dru."

"No sense in it."

"I want to see her, anyhow," Johnny said. "I'll saddle a horse, cross the bridge, and find her. Forget about me, Pache."

"I can forget you," Pache said. "But Ben won't. You want to live, start traveling."

Johnny saddled a horse. He rode across the bridge to the main house, dismounted, and swung toward the door. It was open and there were no lights inside, but a woman stepped out. He guessed instantly it was Syl.

She guessed his name, too. She said, "Johnny Lang?"

"That's right," Johnny nodded.

Her voice was harsh. "Did you kill him?"

"No?"

"Why not?"

He was recovering from his surprise. Staring at her narrowly, he wondered why she was so bitter, so harsh. "It just didn't work out that way," he said slowly. "Besides, I don't go around shooting folks. If you want someone like that, get Shadow Wells or Kelso."

She reached up to touch her hair in an unconscious gesture. "Where are you going?"

"I don't know."

She surprised him again. "Take me with you."

"Wouldn't be a comfortable place," Johnny said. "Where I'll be riding, we might be running into a cloud of bullets, almost anytime. I want to see Dru."

"Why?"

"I just want to see her—talk to her. Where is she?"

"Locked in her room."

"Take me there."

"I don't see why," Syl said. "In fact, I don't understand you at all. Why don't you want to take me with you? Did you ever look at me?"

Her voice had softened. Her manner was a duplicate of the pose she had used to persuade Ben not to hang Johnny. It implied a promise of herself and of her body.

"It's like this," Johnny said slowly. "There

are times when a man's got a job to do—and nothing else can get in the way. Not food, not rest—not even a woman. You've got the sense to understand that. Now, take me to Dru."

She sounded teasing. "Just to talk."

"Yes. Just to talk."

She hesitated, but finally nodded. "All right, Johnny. But I'm going with you. I'll be listening to everything you say."

She led him inside, across a darkened parlor, and several steps along a corridor. At one of the doors, she stopped.

"This it?" Johnny asked.

"Yes, but I don't have a key. You'll have to break in."

Johnny raised his voice. "You in there, Dru? Keep away from the door."

He lunged against the panels. On the third try, the door broke in. Inside, a lamp on a table was burning, and in its light he saw Dru. She was lying on the bed, her wrists and ankles tied to the bedposts.

"I thought you might find me," she said, and her smile was forced. She didn't look good, either. Her face looked tired. There was a scratch across her forehead and a dark bruise on her cheek. Her blouse was torn at the shoulder.

"Who did it?" Johnny asked, stepping to the bed to release her.

"The men who brought me here," Dru answered.

"I had left my door open, expecting no one but you. Instead, two of my father's riders came in. They said Ben Mohegan wanted to see me. If I hadn't fought, they might not have hurt me."

"You were tied up when I walked in."

"That's because I said I wouldn't stay."

"How did Mohegan find out who you were?"

"I told him. We had a rather nasty scene. It didn't help."

"Why was he keeping you?"

"I think he didn't know what else to do with me. I defied him. I told him what I meant to do—to pull him down—to destroy him. At first he laughed, but after a while he was shouting at me, threatening me. Then she came in."

Her hands were free now. She was sitting up on the edge of the bed, pointing to Syl.

"Of course I came in," Syl said. "I was curious about you. I didn't know Ben had a daughter."

"He didn't know, either," Dru said. "Or maybe he had forgotten. At first, he didn't believe I was his daughter." She switched her attention to Johnny. "Where is he now? How did you get in? And where are his men?"

"That's too many questions," Johnny said. He looked over at Syl. "Where are the men?"

"From what I heard, some rancher on the south Flats moved his cattle on Ben's land. Ben ordered his men to drive the cattle back where they belonged."

"Good. That might take quite a long time," Johnny said. "Now what do you two women want to do."

"I'm more interested in what you're going to do," Dru said.

Johnny scowled back. That was a good question. What was he going to do? "What's it to be, Johnny?" Dru said, leaning forward. "The offer I made before is still there."

He shook his head definitely. "No, Dru. I'm still not interested. If I've got a quarrel with your father, it's my own quarrel. I'll fight it my own way. In a few minutes, I'll be leaving. While I take care of something I neglected, you and Syl decide what you want."

He swung away, left the room, walked outside and headed back across the bridge. No one seemed to be about, but by this time, Pache Yates should have packed his belongings and left.

Johnny turned toward the barn. He stumbled across Ben Mohegan's body stretched out just inside the door. The man was groaning, giving indications of waking up. With a length of rope, Johnny tied the man's wrists and ankles. He took time to do a good job. Then he dragged the body outside and left it in the middle of the yard.

Back in the main house, he faced the two women. They had been talking while he was away, and had made a decision. Dru Mohegan spoke for them. “We want to get away,” she said bluntly. “I can go to town. I’ll be safe there. But that won’t do for Syl. She’ll have to go farther. Maybe you can help her.”

“I didn’t think you wanted me to leave, Dru,” Johnny said.

“I don’t. But what’ll we do about Syl? The only sure way to escape would be through the hills. Syl might not make it alone.”

Johnny took a brief turn around the room. He stopped, facing Syl. “Do you know your way to Howie Fry’s? It’s up on Ute Flats.”

She shook her head. “I’ve never been there. I’ve never been anywhere excepting to town. Besides, I don’t want to stay somewhere in the valley. I’d be found. I want to get away.”

“In a direct chase, you might get caught. Howie could hide you for a time. It’s the only safe course to follow. I wish you knew where he lives.”

Dru spoke up. “I know where he lives. I could take her.”

“It would be wise for you to go there too,” Johnny said, swinging toward her. “What makes you think you’d be safe in town?”

“Maybe I wouldn’t be,” Dru said, and she was twisting her hands together. “All right, I’ll go to Howie’s. You’ll have to get us horses.”

As Johnny was leading the horses through the yard to the bridge, Ben Mohegan shouted at him, then cursed him when he didn’t stop.

Ben was awake, but the rope held him fast.

In front of the main house, the two women were ready to ride. "What do we say to Howie?" Dru asked.

Johnny hesitated. It suddenly occurred to him that in sending the two women to Howie Fry, he might be presuming a great deal. He hadn't seen Howie in five years. In that space of time, a man could change—but that seemed unlikely. The Howie he remembered had been a firebrand, too reckless for his own good. He never had liked Ben Mohegan, and he wouldn't have changed. Surely, if anyone around here was fighting Mohegan, he was one.

"You might tell Howie, hello," he said, grinning. "Then, say anything you wish about yourself, or Syl. And tell Howie I want him to hide you. Suggest that he send you to the cliff ruins we found long ago. I doubt if Ben Mohegan ever heard of them."

"When will we see you?"

"I'll get there soon as I can."

She leaned toward him. "Can I ask what you're going to do."

"I haven't decided."

Syl reined toward him. "You won't forget me, Johnny? I'm not sure I want to go to any Indian ruins. What would I do?"

"Maybe you should have packed your knitting?" Johnny said.

• • •

After they had disappeared in the darkness and the sounds of their horses had vanished, Johnny had a cigaret. After he finished he dropped it, stepped on it, then returned across the bridge to where Ben Mohegan was lying. The man heard him coming, and greeted him with a question. "Who were those horses for?"

"One for your daughter, and one for Syl," Johnny replied. "They're gone. You'll never see them again."

"The hell I won't," Mohegan shouted. "I don't care where they go, I'll find them."

"It's a big world."

"I'll still find them."

"You won't have time. The wolf pack around you will keep you busy."

"Those men on the bench and up on the flats—hell with them. I'll smash 'em in a week."

"Maybe, or maybe you won't," Johnny said. "But what I want to talk about now is us. I owe you something, Mohegan."

"Then shoot me, and get it over with."

"That isn't what you were going to do with me. You were going to flog me, and then hang me."

"By God, you had earned it."

Johnny shook his head. "No. You're wrong. When I lived here, I stood up against you. Once I held up one of your men, but only to keep him from buying a bull we wanted. I was returning the money when I was arrested. That cost me five years in prison."

"You were a thief. You said you meant to return the money. That's a lie."

"No, it wasn't a lie. But to go on, when I got out of prison I came back. But not to see you or to cause you any trouble."

"The hell you didn't. You shot my nephew."

"Where is he? Not here. Probably he's riding with your men. He wasn't hurt badly at all, but you got Henry Ashe to head a posse to ride me down."

"Will might have died."

"You knew he wouldn't die—but you hoped I would. Mohegan, I can't understand you. I wanted to leave you alone, but you wouldn't let me. I didn't want to hit back, but I've got to. I've got to think about myself."

"Then shoot me, Lang. You'd better. If I ever get free, I'll finish the job I started."

Johnny was silent for a moment. He stared hard at Mohegan, trying to analyze the man. He seemed to have no fear. He was bound, and at the mercy of an enemy, but he didn't appear at all rattled. It might have been courage which held him up, but Johnny didn't think so. Most likely, Mohegan knew that while he was bound and helpless, he was in no physical danger.

"I wish Pache hadn't hit you," Johnny said.

"We would have been forced to settle things in the barn."

"Give me my gun now," Mohegan challenged.

Johnny straightened, shaking his head. "I'd like to, but shooting it out isn't enough anymore. Just lie where you are, Mohegan. Watch what happens."

He swung away, recrossed the bridge, and entered the main house. Then, room by room, he searched the place. From the rear rooms he routed the servants, ordering them outside. After that he went through the house again, this time building a dozen fires. When this had been done, he rode away, heading east toward Crows' Bench. Behind him, a red glow blossomed from the earth. It spread its glow into the sky. For three hours, Johnny would be able to see it.

# VIII

George Haspwell was in his early fifties. A tall, raw-boned man—gruff and unfriendly in his manner. For years, Johnny had been uneasy in his presence, but he had gradually come to realize that Haspwell's attitude wasn't a forbidding thing. It was a protective shell against the world. Once he got inside it, he found the man was just like anyone else.

It was noon of the next day when Johnny rode up to the Haspwell ranch. This was a well-remembered place. He had been here many times, to take Merth home, or to stop for the evening. He knew the house almost as well as his own.

Haspwell came out on the porch as he rode in, recognized him, and walked into the yard to meet him. He seemed glad to see him, yet there was something reserved in his manner. He said, "Nice to see you, Johnny. Come inside and eat."

He called his wife, then took charge of Johnny's horse while Johnny walked toward Mrs. Haspwell. She was a thin, pleasant looking woman, still young in appearance. She welcomed him with a wide smile.

"We hoped you would stop by," she told him. And then she added quickly, "We saw Merth in town yesterday. I'm glad you saw her."

She was looking at him and her eyes were suddenly anxious. She had known, of course, that he and Merth had planned to get married, and it must have worried her how he would take it that Merth had married someone else.

"Certainly I saw her," Johnny said. "She seemed as beautiful as ever."

He made the words light, and Doris Haspwell seemingly reassured, rewarded him by relaxing.

George Haspwell joined them and they went inside. After dinner, they sat at the table and talked. Haspwell had two men working for him, but both were away.

"Isn't one of your men named Rawles?" Johnny asked.

"Yes. Do you know him?" Haspwell inquired.

"No, I don't think I do," Johnny admitted. "But didn't Rich Gilmore, or Merth, talk to you about him."

"Not to me," Haspwell said. "Why should he? Lin Rawles is one of the best men I ever had. What are you driving at?"

"Maybe it's nothing," Johnny said. "Or if it is, one of them will mention it some other time. Forget it. Tell me what you've been doing. You both look well."

They went on talking, and Johnny tried to put Lin Rawles out of his mind. But it seemed like a strange thing that Merth or Rich hadn't talked to Haspwell. That night at the line shack, the men bursting in had known he was there. Someone had told them, and Rich Gilmore indirectly had blamed Lin Rawles. Unless he had changed his mind, he should have said something.

They got to the matter of Ben Mohegan all too soon, but that probably couldn't be helped. Right now, nothing else was so important. A fight was shaping up in the valley, and some of those along the bench and over on the flats were getting impatient.

"We're having a secret meeting tomorrow night," Haspwell said. "It'll be at Carl Macey's. I hope you can be there."

Johnny shook his head. "Don't count on me."

"But why not?" Haspwell demanded. "Who has more reasons than you to hate him? You've got to be on our side, Johnny."

"No, Haspwell. Your fight with Mohegan isn't mine. I do have a matter to settle with him, but it's a private quarrel. It has nothing to do with roads, cattle markets, or county government."

"You could throw in with us. We'd all like to have you. I'm sure of it."

"Sure. I'm one more gun."

The man looked hurt. "Don't put it that way, Johnny. At least, come to the meeting tomorrow night."

"Too risky."

"I told you it was a secret meeting. Nothing to worry about."

"But there you're wrong," Johnny said. "If one man tells something to another, it's no longer a secret. At least a dozen men know of the meeting. Their wives probably know. And some of the men riding for them. You might as well post a notice in town. Someone'll talk."

The man bit his lips. "We've got to trust each other. How else can we work together. I know it's true, someone might talk. But we'll post guards. We won't be surprised if Mohegan raids us."

Johnny got up. He started pacing the room, shaking his head. After a moment he stopped at the table and stood scowling at George Haspwell. "I don't like this range war," he said flatly. "I don't like it because any way you handle it, too many people will get hurt. I don't like it because the odds are uneven. Mohegan's got a crowd of gunslingers, men who live by their guns. They fight dirty. You wouldn't want to shoot a man in the back; Mohegan's men will. To whip a man like Mohegan, you've got to get as dirty as he is. You've got to smother your conscience. You've got to do some ugly things. If you do you might win, but at the end your hands will be bloody—and the blood won't wipe off."

During the rest of the day, Johnny caught some sleep in Haspwell's barn. Haspwell woke him at dusk and he was half apologetic. "You were dead to the world. Hated to bother you. Had a notion to post a guard and let you rest until morning."

"It's good you didn't," Johnny said. "We might have been interrupted."

He felt loggy and stiff. He got up, stretched, and then scrubbed his jaw. He needed another shave.

"Lin Rawles rode in a few minutes ago," Haspwell said. "He's been in town. Heard a few things. Seems there was a fire last night at the Double M. Ben Mohegan's house burned to the ground. Didn't save a thing. Not a stick of furniture. They're blaming it on you."

Johnny nodded. "Sure . . . Got a razor I can use?"

"As I got the story, two men were killed. Tex Tyler and a man named Parrish."

"Where do I get a razor?"

Haspwell showed a sudden flash of anger. "All right, I'll get you a razor. And I don't mind the death of two gunslingers. But to burn down a house—suppose Ben Mohegan starts to burn us out—just to get even."

"You can always rebuild," Johnny said quietly. "Think about it for a minute. Money and possessions aren't important. They can be replaced. Life is another matter. Take a man's life—you can't give it back."

Haspwell ran his fingers through his hair. "Maybe you're right. But I wish you hadn't burned that house. Mohegan was proud of it. Now, the fat's in the fire, for sure."

"Wasn't it before? I told you already, Haspwell. A fight's an ugly thing."

"I'll get your razor," Haspwell said gruffly.

As Johnny shaved by lantern light in the barn, Lin Rawles came in. He was thin, tall, about twenty-five, freckle-faced, and had rusty hair. His grin was impudent, but his voice reflected a tinge of envy. "So you're Johnny Lang. Must have had quite a time at the Double M. What kind of an army helped you?"

"Wish I had had one," Johnny said. "Put it down that I was lucky."

"What's next on the program?"

Johnny interrupted his shaving to look at the man. Merth had said she didn't trust him and Rich Gilmore had suggested that Rawles might be a spy for Mohegan. That was possible, but in spite of such warnings, Johnny was skeptical. He had felt an instinctive liking for the man.

"Do you know the valley?" he asked bluntly. "Mohegan's land?"

"Part of it," Rawles nodded.

"Where's Mohegan's winter grazing land?"

"Off toward the flats. What you thinking about?"

"Haystacks. They burn easy."

"Need a helper?"

"Now wait a minute," Haspwell broke in. "You can't do a thing like that, Johnny. We all got hay stored for the winter. If you start more fires—"

"Then guard them," Johnny said. "Or let them go."

"We'll need that hay for winter feed."

"You can always buy winter feed."

"Johnny, I don't like it."

Johnny shrugged. Outside, he noticed it was nearly dark. He had to eat, but if he left immediately afterwards, he should be able to get across the valley before dawn.

"We'll go in and have supper," Haspwell said. "And after that, Johnny, I want to talk to you."

"Won't do any good," Johnny said. "To be honest, I think Mohegan's going to be too busy to worry about your hay. He's got me on his mind. And Pache Yates. Syl, too. Syl's run away from him."

"I still don't like it," Haspwell muttered.

"How about me?" Lin Rawles insisted.

Johnny looked at him curiously. "Why?"

"Let me put it this way," the man answered. "Been here a couple years. At first, it wasn't too bad, but for months now a man takes his life in his hands when he goes to town. The place is flooded with Mohegan's gunslingers. Hard to keep out of their way. We been talking about doing something, but until you showed up, no one did anything. When you got to face a problem, I'm for facing it."

"And you don't mind getting shot."

"Sure I would. But I could get killed anytime. In fact, next time I run into Kelso that might happen. I've heard he was after me. He's one of Mohegan's men."

"I've heard of him," Johnny nodded, and then he glanced at George Haspwell.

"I need Rawles here at the ranch," Haspwell said definitely.

That seemed to settle the matter. They had supper, and following that, Johnny rode away, taking the road to the valley. He was only a few miles away, however, when he heard somcone pounding up behind him. It was Lin Rawles.

The man grinned as he reined up. "Haspwell decided he could get along without me."

"I'll bet you ducked out on your own," Johnny answered.

"At least, I'm here. Packed along some grub, too."

Johnny squinted at the man. What Merth and Rich had said still worried him, and after a moment he asked, "Rawles, did you tell Rich Gilmore the way to your line shack, up in the hills."

"Nope. We don't do much talking. Don't get along."

"Why?"

Rawles was scowling. “Maybe he’s a friend of yours, and maybe he’s all right, but in my book, he’s got too many faces.”

“How about Merth?”

“I had a fight with her husband. Tried to get me fired. But look here, Johnny. If you don’t want me along, just say so, and I’ll turn back.”

“We’ll ride on,” Johnny said.

They hit five haystacks before dawn and set them afire. After burning the last one, they slanted southeast to Georgia Creek. Then, under the screen of the trees and shrubbery lining the stream, they headed toward town. At mid-morning, however, and at a point where they were well covered, they made a temporary camp, and had something to eat.

Off toward the flats the five burning haystacks sent columns of smoke into the sky. Until evening, the fires would continue,

“That smoke was noticed right after dawn,” Lin Rawles guessed. “By now, a crowd of Mohegan’s men are hunting for us. Sure hope we blinded our trail.”

“We might have to start running any minute,” Johnny said. “Or we might be entirely safe.”

“Mohegan’s going to be raving.”

“That’s what I’m counting on. The burning of a few haystacks isn’t really very important. Mohegan’s got the money to buy winter feed. But the defiance of invading his land and of not being able to hit back will hurt. We could shoot half of Mohegan's men. He'd just hire more. But if we hit his property, he'll scream. It's a damned strange thing to realize that property is more important than people."

"To George Haspwell, too. If you asked him, he would say people are more important than property. But in the fight again, he wasn't worried about who got hurt. He was worried his house and his hay might get burned. To hell with him."

"You don't have any property," Johnny said dryly.

"You mean, I'd be like that too?"

"Wouldn't you?"

Lin Rawles was scowling. "I don't know. Never thought about it. Maybe I would."

"At least, I've finished for the morning. We'll stay here for a time, if we can. I'll grab a couple hours of sleep while you watch. Then it'll be your turn."

The day passed uneventfully. Johnny slept until well into the afternoon. Lin slept until dusk. By now, Johnny was thinking of him by that name, and as well as he could judge, he couldn't have been Mohegan's spy. He just wasn't that type.

They rode on at dusk, still heading toward town, and by ten that evening, reined up in sight of the blinking lights.

"If all you want is news, no sense in you going

in," Lin said. "Why don't I go. No one's after me—yet."

"How about Kelso," Johnny suggested.

"Might not be there. Good chance he's chasing ghosts here and there across the valley."

Johnny laughed. He said, "All right, Lin. Go on in to town. Pick up whatever information you can, but don't be foolish. If Kelso's around, dodge him."

Lin Rawles was gone for nearly an hour, but in that space of time he had learned a great deal. Hunkering down on the ground in a clearing on Georgia Creek just above town, he made his report. Ben Mohegan, apparently, had moved his headquarters to Georgia City, and had established himself in a house next to the barber shop, where Edith Brooks had lived. What had happened to her, Lin didn't know. The reward posted on Johnny's head had been increased to a thousand dollars. Where he was, no one seemed to know, and in an effort to find him, Mohegan had split his men into a number of small groups, ranging up and down the valley. Exactly where they were searching wasn't certain. A town posse, headed by Henry Ashe, was ready to go wherever needed.

One man had told Lin that Mohegan's wife had perished in the fire of the Double M ranch house. Another rumor was that she had been sent to visit friends until the trouble here was over. And rather interestingly, there had been a shooting in town, just after noon—a duel between Ben Mohegan and Pache Yates. Pache had been killed.

"I don't know what the trouble was," Lin said. "But it's a lucky thing for us. If Pache had been trailing us, we'd have a crowd at our heels right now."

Johnny made no comment about that, but he was amazed at Pache's death. Surely he could have fled from the valley. He had started to. Then he must have changed his mind, and gone to town to await Mohegan's arrival. Perhaps he had thought they could talk. Or maybe he had known he would be killed, but had chosen to do that rather than run. Johnny probably never would know the truth.

"Does this help any?" Lin asked.

"A great deal," Johnny answered. "Do you have any wire cutters in your saddle bags?"

"Several at the ranch. None here."

"Know where you could get some."

"Think so. Where we going to use them?"

"Mohegan's got a south fence, beyond Georgia creek. We passed several large herds just above the fence this morning. Mohegan wouldn't like to lose them."

Lin was grinning. "So we're going to turn rustler, huh?"

"They'll hang us anyhow—if they catch us. Does it bother you?"

“Not too much,” Lin answered, getting to his feet. “Be back, soon as I can.”

Lin wasn’t gone long. He returned with two pairs of wire cutters—and more information. Disturbing information. “Just as I was leaving town three of Mohegan’s men rode in with a prisoner. Didn’t take him to jail. Took him instead to the house where Mohegan’s living.

“Who was it?” Johnny asked.

“Howie Fry.”

Johnny stiffened. He stared in the direction of the town.

“Don’t know why they picked on Howie, but maybe it was in the cards,” Lin said. “He’s been one of the leaders of the pack fighting Mohegan.”

Johnny nodded. That might have been one of the reasons why Howie Fry had been brought in. But there could be another. The two women who had fled from the Double M had gone to Howie. Mohegan’s men might have trailed them. But that wasn’t all he had to worry about. More immediately, Howie had been delivered into Mohegan’s hands, and Mohegan liked to use his whip.

# IX

It was a dark night, but Johnny wished it had been darker. Too many stars were out. The shadows were too thin. He stared toward the town, picturing the interior of Dru's house.

"If we're going to cut any fences, we ought to get started," Lin said.

Johnny squinted at the man. "Those wire cutters you brought looked new."

"They were new. Took them from Ed Romig's store. Went in through a back window. Someday, I'll pay him."

"Does Romig handle dynamite?"

"Sure does."

"Can you handle it?"

"Yep. What do you want to blow up?"

"The bank ought to do," Johnny said slowly. "We won't rob it, but for a few minutes we want everyone in town to think the bank is being blasted open. While the folks are worrying about the bank, I'll pick up Howie."

Lin's eyes had narrowed. "You better tell me more. Ben Mohegan must have eight or nine men in town. We make two."

"We'll try this," Johnny said slowly. "You go to Ed Romig's. Pick up several sticks of dynamite, circle to the side of the bank, light the dynamite, and pitch it through the window. The blast ought to draw everyone outside. While people are closing in on the bank, I'll walk into Mohegan's and pick up Howie. After you get rid of the dynamite, grab an extra horse, and meet us west of town."

From the edge of town, Johnny hurried in the direction of Dru's house. Then, from the side of the shed behind it, he stared at the building.

He stepped forward and he hurried to the back corner of the building. No one challenged him. From there, he crept slowly along the side of the house, and finally, flat on his stomach, he reached the front corner of the porch. Raising his head, Johnny now could see part of the main street. At the tie-rail directly ahead were five saddle horses. More were up in front of Jourdan's. He couldn't see the bank. It was on this side of the street, but out of sight.

It hadn't taken him many minutes to get here, and if Lin Rawles worked fast, he wouldn't have to wait long.

Johnny checked his gun, made sure he had his pocket knife, and then waited. The minutes piled up. Too many of them. Johnny raised his head to look up and down the street. Everything seemed quiet, but Lin might have run into trouble. He might not have been able to get the dynamite. Maybe—

The blast of the dynamite startled him—even though he had been waiting for it. It was a heavy blast that seemed to shake the earth. The deafening sound rolled over him like a wave. Then, in its echoes, Johnny heard men shouting. Some of the shouting came from up and down the street, but some of it also came from the men bursting out of Dru's. Two men pounded across the porch to the street. Three more followed. Then another—Ben Mohegan. He stopped just outside the door and looked back. He motioned with his arm. "Stay there and guard the prisoner," he shouted. "Be right back."

Someone in the street was shouting that the bank had been blasted. Ben Mohegan raced that way, and as he disappeared, Johnny got to his feet. He drew his gun, stepped to the porch, and hurried to the door. There could be no hesitation now. This was the moment to pick up Howie Fry, whether he had one guard, or a dozen.

Johnny swung through the door. He almost ran into a man blocking his way. The man was there, probably just to look outside, but his gun was in his hand, and when he saw Johnny he stepped back and started to raise the gun. Only he didn't get to use it. Johnny's bullet hit him in the chest, driving him backwards.

As the man fell, Johnny took a sweeping glance at the room. Howie Fry was there, bound and lying on the floor. Two other men were there, too. They had been at the window, trying to see what was happening up the street at the bank. But they weren't doing that now. The shooting in the doorway had caught their attention. They were swinging toward Johnny, jerking up their guns.

Johnny threw a shot at the man who was closest. Then, he switched his aim to shoot at the other. A blow hit him in the side. It staggered him. He saw that one of the men was down, but the other was still on his feet. The man had fired once, and had been knocked sideways by a bullet, but was steadying his arm to shoot again. Johnny drove another bullet at the man and saw him arch backward, then pitch to the floor.

Howie Fry had managed to sit up. He was as thin and boney as Johnny remembered. He gasped, "Johnny! Johnny Lang! I don't believe it."

"Like to get out of here?" Johnny asked.

"Would I—damned right I would. Cut me free and give me a gun."

"I'll cut you free, but we're going to run," Johnny said. "No sense in dying while you're still young."

"Better get me a gun," Howie insisted. "Won't take Mohegan long to figure out what's happened."

Johnny shook his head. "Got to get you free, first."

"Who blew up the town?"

"Man I picked up—Lin Rawles."

"Couldn't have done better. Saw on those ropes faster."

Johnny was doing the best he could to cut the ropes, but the pain stabbing through his body made him dizzy. He had been hit in the side, several inches above the waist. The bullet had gone all the way through, and he was losing blood from both openings. He could feel it soaking down his leg.

Howie noticed it. "Johnny—you've been hit. I didn't know."

"Not bad," Johnny said. "Forget it."

He finally finished sawing through the ropes around Howie's ankles and stood up, weaving uncertainly from side to side.

Howie scrambled to his feet. He got a gun from the hand of one of the men who had been shot, took a quick look through the front door, then hurried to Johnny's side. "They're on their way here—just outside. Swing around. We got a fight on our hands."

"No. Take the back door," Johnny insisted. "Lin's getting a horse you can use. Tonight we can't win. Tomorrow may be different."

He was pointing to the rear. Howie hesitated. He probably had suffered as a prisoner, but now he had a gun and he wanted to use it. He didn't however. "Got to get you out of here," he said. "All right, we'll run."

He slipped his arm around Johnny's shoulders and helped him toward the rear of the house.

The pain in Johnny's side was getting worse. His dizziness had increased. He had only vague memories of escaping from Dru's house. He thought they got outside without any trouble, but as they went through the yard, someone started shooting at them. Howie fired back. Then, surprisingly, Lin Rawles showed up and joined in the battle.

It didn't last long, however. Soon they were hurrying through the darkness, and after a time they came to a horse, the one Lin had secured for Howie. They gave the horse to Johnny, however, but after they boosted him into the saddle, he lost consciousness.

That was the first time he passed out. The first of a dozen times of sliding into the shadows, then to awaken. Sometimes when he awoke he was weaving in his saddle, tied so he wouldn't fall. Sometimes he was lying on a blanket, under the trees. Sometimes it was dark; sometimes the sun was shining.

He was troubled by weird, fantastic dreams. Twice he awoke to a conscious state which he knew was real, and in which he remembered the gun fight in Dru's house in Georgia City, the wound in his side, and his escape accompanied by Howie Fry and Lin Rawles. The first time that happened he was alone, and it was night, and it struck him that he had been abandoned somewhere. He tried to get up, but the effort dragged him back into the blackness. The second time, someone was with him, and from her voice it was a woman. Her hands were cool and gentle, but she made him drink something bitter which made him gag. He wanted to talk to her but he was suddenly tired, and he must have gone to sleep.

He awoke a third time, and stooping over him was Dru Mohegan. She was looking at him anxiously, her eyes dark and steady. Her voice was hushed. "Hello, Johnny. Welcome back to the world."

"Have I been away?" he asked, puzzled.

"For at least three days," Dru answered. "A hundred times I've stooped over you, and been sure you were dead. But I was wrong. Now don't get worried. You're going to get well. Just lie there, and don't talk."

"Where are we?" Johnny insisted. "I want to know."

"All right, I'll tell you," Dru said. "But you mustn't ask any more questions until you are stronger. We are in a hunting cabin, up in the Sandoval mountains. Howie built it two years ago. No one else has ever been up here. He thought it was a better hiding place for us than the old Indian ruins. Others have been there."

"Is Syl—"

"Syl is here, but right now she's at a lookout post with Lin Rawles. Howie Fry left this morning. He's gone to get some meat. He wants to make some broth for you. Besides, our supplies are getting rather low. Howie'll be back in the morning."

There were a dozen questions in Johnny's mind, but he was suddenly too tired to ask them. Dru Mohegan, however, still was talking, and Johnny listened.

"The wound in your side isn't bad. It's healing nicely. Both openings are closed and the swelling and the redness around it is fading. What nearly took your life was the blood you lost. When Howie and Lin carried you in, I don't think they could have squeezed another drop out of you. They said they tried to stop the bleeding—and they did—but every time you had to move, the bleeding started again. And for three days they were trying to get you here. So it's six days since you were shot. Almost a week. And you've eaten scarcely a thing. When Howie gets back . . ."

She was still talking, but her voice seemed farther and farther away, and finally Johnny couldn't hear it. He had gone to sleep again.

The next day Johnny felt better, and from then on, his recovery was rapid. He developed a ravenous appetite. He didn't want to stay in bed.

Howie Fry returned with supplies, and now with Johnny feeling better and wanting to move around, he made another trip to the valley, this time after information. The word he brought back was disturbing. Out on the range, there had been no definite clash between Mohegan and the fringing ranchers, but in Georgia City, there had been half-a-dozen incidents. Several of them serious. A man working for Carl Macey, and another employed by Abe Buell, had been killed. Vern Waddington, one of the Crows' Bench ranchers, had been badly beaten. But that was only part of the story.

"As I figure it, it's like this," Howie said. "Since Ben Mohegan's ranch house was burned, he's moved his headquarters to town. He keeps some of his men on the run, hunting for us, but a good part of the time a crowd of his men are stalking the streets. They drink too much. They're troublesome. A woman ain't safe outside, anymore. And none of the fringe ranchers or their men dare to come to town."

"What do folks do for supplies?" Johnny asked.

"I reckon they're doing without. Talked to Brad Ellsworth, down on the flats. He says he figures he would be taking his life in his hands if he rode to town—and it ain't worth it to take the risk. Carl Macey sent a letter to Santa Fe, asking for a federal marshal, but who knows when we'll get any action."

"Time for me to do something," Johnny said slowly.

"You mean, us," Lin Rawles said. "You ain't in shape to do any hard riding, Johnny."

"He's right," Howie said. "You see, it's like this, Johnny. Mohegan's sure you haven't left. He's waiting for you to show up. Once you do, he'll send every man he's got after you. They won't stop until they ride you down."

"It might happen that way," Johnny conceded.

He felt his side. It still pained him. He hadn't recovered his full strength. In two or three days he would feel better but who knew what might happen in two or three days.

"Johnny, when we move, what do you want to do?" Howie asked. "We're not strong enough to face Ben Mohegan."

"There are lots of ways to fight a man," Johnny said. "It hurt Mohegan to lose his wife. Syl left of her own choice, but we got credit. Then it hurt Mohegan to lose his house. It hurt him to lose five haystacks."

Howie sounded disgusted. "What's five haystacks? What's even a house."

"We defied him, Howie. We laughed at him. Men like Ben Mohegan can't stand it if they're laughed at."

"And that's the way you mean to fight him?"

"That's right," Johnny nodded. "Mohegan has a barn we can burn. He has more haystacks which can be destroyed. He had several herds near his south fence. If we start them into the badlands,

Mohegan will have to send men after them. Then, there's another step we should take, but it's rather risky. I want to think about it."

"When'll we ride? Two or three days?" Lin asked.

"We'll leave in the morning," Johnny said.

In general, Dru did the cooking and Syl handled the cleanup work. That evening, however, Syl disappeared soon after supper, and Dru was left with the job. Lying on his bunk, Johnny watched her. "What happened to Syl?" he asked abruptly.

"It's a nice evening," Dru answered. "I suppose she is sitting outside."

"With Lin Rawles?"

"Maybe. He's a rather nice person. And don't say anything about Syl. Since I've got to know her, I rather like her. I know she married my father because of his money, but at least she had the courage to leave him. She hasn't had an easy life."

"Do you know something, Dru?" Johnny said. "What you've discovered about Syl, you could learn from anyone else."

"You mean, to know people is to like them."

"That's right, Dru. Maybe it doesn't work always, but usually it does. I think you might even like your father—if you really knew him."

She stiffened instantly. "How can you say that. I know my father."

"But how well do you know him? You were only twelve when you left the valley. A girl of twelve couldn't have had mature judgment. If I had to make a guess, your opinion of your father was a combination of two things. Your memory of his harshness—and what your mother told you about him. And she was bitter—possibly with cause—but still bitter."

She looked at him curiously. "Why are you saying that? You can't like him?"

"I'm trying to understand him. He took this valley as a young man. Maybe he had to drive out a few people to get it, but for years he's been wealthy. He's had all the money, cattle and land he needed. . . . Then why is he like he is—bitter and hard, cruel, sadistic, ready for a quarrel any day?"

"You tell me," Dru said, and she snapped out the words.

"I can tell you what Pache Yates said—and it was rather interesting. This wasn't any final summation. It was just a casual statement, but here it is. Ben Mohegan never had the wife he wanted. He had money, land, cattle, a fine house but no one to fill it. In Pache's word, *Ben never had no luck with his women. His first wife cried all the time. His second nagged him. Syl was the third, and I'm sure Syl gave him little real satisfaction.*"

Dru was silent for a moment, frowning, then

she wiped her hands, and walked toward him. "I don't want to talk about it."

"All right, Dru," Johnny agreed.

"Excepting this," Dru said. "I think I owe you ten thousand dollars."

He shook his head, grinning. "I've never listened to your proposition, and I never will. How about a new dressing on my side?"

"Right away," Dru said.

As she did that, Johnny watched her face. She was two people. When she was talking about her father, or thinking of him, her body would get rigid, her facc would freeze up, and she looked at least forty. At other times she could laugh, her eyes might sparkle, and color would show in her cheeks. On such occasions he was reminded quite definitely that she was a woman, and so completely desirable that it made him uneasy.

A vagrant thought crossed his mind. He mentioned it aloud. "I suppose Syl and Lin Rawles are making love."

Her lips twitched. "Don't be prudish. Why shouldn't they? They're not children."

"Neither are we," Johnny said.

She stepped away quickly, her face scarlet, her breathing suddenly fast. She spoke under her breath. "You didn't mean that, Johnny."

"Look at me."

"No."

"Look at me."

She shook her head and twisted her hands together. She tried to make her voice light. "Don't think about me, Johnny. I'm not a woman. I'm just a bundle of emotions, all of them ugly. I'm filled up inside—filled with hate."

Johnny shook his head. "I don't believe you."

"You can prove it."

"How?"

She turned away, her hands now clenched at her sides. "Here is the test, Johnny. Right now, probably, Syl is trying to persuade Lin not to ride with you tomorrow. She doesn't want him killed. I don't want you to get killed, either, but I can hardly wait for you to ride. Even if I knew it would cost your life, I wouldn't try to stop you. Now what do you think of me?"

"I don't think you mean what you say," Johnny said.

"But I do—I do. I wish—"

Her voice broke. She whirled away and hurried from the room, stumbling as she neared the door.

# X

They saddled up the next morning, just after dawn. Howie Fry had made a scouting trip the previous evening, and reported that as nearly as he could tell, the way to the valley was open. Dru and Syl would remain in the cabin. Howie had brought in supplies which should carry them for at least ten days.

It took them all day to drop down through the mountains to the rugged hills above Ute Flats. They could have made the trip much faster, but this time, in particular, they had wanted to blind their trail. In the next day or so, Mohegan would learn they were back, and undoubtedly, some of his men would pick up their trail and try to backtrack.

At about midnight they hit one of the creeks which would lead them to the Sandoval River. There they camped. They remained until late the next afternoon. The rest was worthwhile—and it was all they might have for some time. Johnny couldn't guess exactly what was ahead, but as soon as Mohegan learned they were back, they couldn't expect much peace.

The servants Mohegan had had at his ranch house had disappeared, but three men had been left at the bunkhouse. They surprised them, disarmed them, bound them, carried them some distance away, and then fired the bunkhouse and the barn. In the next two hours, they set fire to three haystacks, north and west of the ranch. From there, riding hard, the three men headed south. By morning, they had cut Mohegan's south fence in a dozen places, and had started three of his herds in a drift toward the badlands. In several days, without being driven, the cattle wouldn't go far. But if Mohegan waited that long he would need a dozen men and a week's work to get the cattle back where they belonged.

"Not a bad night's work," Howie said as the sun came up. "Where do we go from here?"

They were south of the valley and south and west of Georgia City by at least four hours. They had been slanting east in open country. At the moment, no other riders were in sight, but they couldn't count on not being followed.

"I think there ought to be a spring down here somewhere," Johnny said. "Seem to remember it."

"Think I could find it," Howie said. "But what then?"

"I like spring water," Johnny said. Then he laughed. "I don't want to get too far from Georgia City. We want to get there tonight, soon after dark as possible."

"What do we do?"

"Do we have any friends in town?"

"That depends," Howie said thoughtfully. "We probably got lots of friends—folks who'd like to see Mohegan smashed. But with Mohegan's men running the town, it takes guts to take sides against him."

They found the spring. It was in a break in the rolling prairie, a shallow, saucer-shaped depression lined by stunted mesquite, pear cactus, and greasewood. Where the water seeped to the surface there was heavier shrubbery. As they rode down to the spring they dropped out of sight of the surrounding plains.

"Of course, this won't save us," Lin said practically. "If Mohegan's men have hit our trail, they'll follow it. It's no secret about this spring. Never been here, but I've heard of it."

"We'll stop to eat and rest," Johnny said. "We'll take turns watching from the rim. If men come in sight, we'll ride on."

They had breakfast, and afterward, Johnny took the first turn watching their back trail. Two hours later, Lin Rawles took his place, and Johnny turned in to take a short nap. It was mid-afternoon when he was wakened. Lin Rawles and Howie Fry both stood above him.

"Company coming?" Johnny asked, sitting up.

"Yep. Four or five riders. Might be six," Howie said. "They're at least two hours behind us."

Johnny got up, stretched, walked to the spring to get a drink, then glanced up at the sky. The sun was three hours high—four hours until dark. That meant they couldn't stay here. To move on, they had to climb up to where they could be seen, and as soon as they came in sight of the riders, the men following them would ride harder.

As they left the spring and turned across country to the northeast, the men following them altered their course to aim straight at them. In the next hour, the distance between them was shortened. But not to any alarming extent. Toward sunset, Mohegan's men were still more than an hour behind them. One rider had left the others, and was cutting to the north, but that was understandable. In that direction lay Georgia City, from where he could summon more men.

Johnny, Lin and Howie stopped briefly to rest their horses and to have a smoke. By now, they were southeast of Georgia City. "Soon as it's dark, we'll cut north until we're above the town, then turn back," Johnny said. "That way, maybe we won't run into a posse leaving town."

Howie nodded. "I've been thinking of who we could depend on once we get there. Some man whose house we could use for a meeting. Most I've thought of have families. But what about Mac Taggart?"

"Didn't he used to run the stage line?"

"Still does. Lives with his wife. Kids are grown." Howie turned to Lin Rawles. "What do you think of Mac?"

"Don't know him very well," Lin answered. "If you think he's all right, we'll try him."

"Did you think of Rich?" Johnny asked.

Howie frowned. "Sure I thought about him—and he might do. He says he's on our side, but he still deals with Mohegan. He says he has to, and maybe that's true. Try him if you want to, but I'd be damned careful."

Johnny pinched out his cigaret. Perhaps Rich Gilmore hadn't betrayed his presence in the line shack. And perhaps Rich had gone out that night in town on an entirely innocent errand. But he couldn't be sure of the man. The only reason he had suggested him had been to get Howie's opinion.

"We'll try Mac Taggart," he decided. "Time to ride on."

After the sun was down and after the evening shadows had thickened, they swung north. Then two hours later, and from a point northeast of town, they cut back. It was shortly after ten when they came in sight of the lights of Georgia City. So far, they had been fortunate; they had run into no other riders. If a posse had left town and headed east, they had missed it.

At a safe distance from the first houses, they reined up, and Johnny turned to Howie. "How well do you know Mac Taggart?"

"Fairly well," Howie replied. "I can ride in first, and talk to him."

Howie was gone for forty-five minutes, but he was grinning when he rejoined them. "It's all set up," he reported. "We can use the house as long as we wish. We can put our horses in Mac's barn. And right now, we don't have to worry too much. Mohegan's left a few men in town, but he and a few others rode out with the sheriff and a posse, to the east, a couple hours ago. They got word that we're aiming toward Crows' Bench. Might be gone until sometime tomorrow."

Mac Taggart was a man of sixty, bald-headed and thin from stomach trouble, but he still stood as straight as when he had been a young soldier on the frontier. His voice was strong, and the clasp of his hand was like the closing of a vise. His smile seemed genuine.

"Glad to meet you again, Johnny," he said. "Always liked your father. Liked you as a youngster. Ain't changed my mind about you, spite of what I've heard lately. Maybe you remember my wife, Gwen."

Mrs. Taggart was a pleasant-looking woman, considerably younger than Taggart. Her hair showed a little gray. She said, "Hello, Johnny," and put out her hand.

"You wanted to see some folks," Taggart said.

"Yes, first I want to see Gil Jourdan," Johnny nodded. "Who runs the other saloon?"

"Shem Kelley, but he only keeps open when he feels like it. Most folks go to Jourdan's."

"Then we'll see Kelley second. Does Mrs. Temple still run the restaurant?"

"Trying to sell it, but she hasn't yet."

"She'll be third—if we have time. Now about Gil Jourdan. Mac, could you bring him outside? Howie and Lin will take it from there."

"Sure, I can do that," Mac agreed.

Johnny paced the room restlessly after Mac, Lin and Howie left to get Jourdan. He knew exactly what he wanted to accomplish, but how well Jourdan would cooperate, he didn't know. And even if he succeeded, it would be a minor victory. It wouldn't hurt Ben Mohegan very much.

After a time, he heard voices outside and whirled to face the door, but it was Mac, Howie and Lin returning with Gil Jourdan.

Jourdan was middle-aged, tall, gaunt, and, against his pale skin, his beard seemed quite heavy. He had deep-shadowed eyes. He looked tired and worried. His voice wasn't steady. "Don't know why I was brought here. I ain't done nothing against you, Lang."

Johnny grinned. "Don't worry, Jourdan. Sit down at the table."

"Got to get back to the saloon, soon as I can," Jourdan said.

"Then we'll rush it," Johnny said. "How much stock do you have."

The saloonkeeper frowned. "Not too much.

Several boxes of whiskey and a barrel of beer. Got more on order. Ought to get in—in a day or so—if Mac's freight wagons don't break down."

"Didn't you used to go fishing?"

"No chance. No help I can trust."

"Then I'll tell you what I want you to do," Johnny said. "Close your saloon, spend the next hour or so burying your whiskey and hiding your barrel of beer. Then pack up some supplies and go fishing. Stay away for the next ten days."

Jourdan looked startled. "What about my saloon?"

"Close it and lock it. Take a vacation."

"Can't afford it."

Johnny shook his head. "You've no choice. Close your saloon, hide your whiskey, and take a vacation. It's either that, Jourdan, or I'll close it myself—with dynamite. And don't worry about Shem Kelley. He's going to close, too."

"But I don't see why—"

"It's a safety measure, Jourdan. Ben Mohegan's moved to town. He's got a dozen men riding with him—hardcases. If some of them get liquored up, who knows who might get shot. Starting tomorrow, both saloons in Georgia City will be closed."

Jourdan shook his head. "Damnit, I can't do it. How can I buck Ben Mohegan? I tell you—"

"Lin," Johnny said, raising his voice. "Have you got the dynamite ready."

"Sure thing," Lin answered. "Half a dozen sticks and we can make Jourdan's look like a smashed matchbox."

"You see, it's like this," Johnny said. "You can lose your saloon and everything inside of it—right tonight. Or you can close up and go away for ten days—and save your business. Now what's it to be?"

Gil Jourdan looked around the room, then his shoulders slumped and he made a mumbling answer. "Reckon I'm goin' fishin'."

Shem Kelley offered even less argument. He didn't like what was happening in Georgia City. He had been uneasy about his customers. If Jourdan was closing, he would be glad to close. By morning, Kelley would be ready to take the stage to Bradentown, where he could visit a son.

Mrs. Temple, who had been operating the restaurant, would be on the same stage, but she would go on to Las Vegas where she had a sister. She didn't mind closing the restaurant. Recently, none of the families from Ute Flats or from Crows' Bench had been coming to town. Her chief customers had been Ben Mohegan and his gunslingers—and their rough manners had disturbed her.

"We might close down a few other things," Mac suggested.

"No, this is enough," Johnny said. "But now we want to see Rich Gilmore. This is the way to set the hook, and to make Ben Mohegan feel it. We want to send him a message. Rich should be able to deliver it."

"He's just too close to Mohegan to suit me," Mac Taggart said. "Want him brought here?"

"No, we'll pay him a visit. I want Merth to hear what we say. Like to have you along, Mac, but it's not necessary."

"Don't mind letting folks know where I stand," Mac said gruffly. "Let's go."

They had to walk across town to get to Rich Gilmore's, and as they reached the main street Johnny heard the sound of horses turning in from the north. But not very many. He signaled to those with him, and they huddled back in the darkness. A moment later, three horsemen came in sight. They glanced at the saloons as they passed, but they didn't notice the signs in the windows. It was quite late, and not strange that the saloons were closed.

The three men reined up in front of the new headquarters set up by Ben Mohegan—the house once occupied by Dru. They dismounted and went inside. Lamplight showed at the windows.

"Probably three men from up valley," Mac whispered. "Mohegan's got several small groups, spotted here and there, watching for you."

"How many were left when the others rode out?" Johnny asked.

"A couple. Maybe three. All told, Mohegan

must have better than twenty men riding for him."

"How many in the sheriff's posse?"

"Not counting Mohegan's men, six or eight. Young fellows from town. Riding for the excitement, or for a chance at the reward money. You're worth a thousand dollars, Johnny. Five hundred for Lin and five hundred for Howie."

Johnny looked up and down the street. At this late hour, most of Georgia City was asleep. Over at Mohegan's there was a light, but the house had been dark before these men arrived. Most probably, the new arrivals would soon go to bed.

"We may drop in there before we leave," Johnny said slowly. "But first, we have to see Rich Gilmore. And we ought to dig up more supplies."

"You can get what you need from our house," Mac Taggart offered. Then he scowled. "Where will you go?"

"Don't know, yet," Johnny said.

"What you need is a hole you can pull in after you," Mac said. "Trouble is, there's no place to hide. And if you run . . ."

Johnny didn't listen to the end of Mac's sentence. Suddenly, he had what they needed. *A hole they could pull in after them.* He laughed softly, then straightened, and said, "Time's running on. We'd better go see Rich Gilmore."

# XI

Rich Gilmore's house was dark. Johnny had to knock several times to get an answer but finally someone came to the door and he heard Rich's voice. The man seemed startled. "Who's there?"

Johnny put his head close to the door. "It's Johnny Lang."

"I'll light the lamp," Rich said. But then he changed his mind. "No, we better not show a light. Someone might notice."

He unbolted the door and opened it. Wearing a long nightgown he looked like a ghost.

"Might as well light the lamp," Johnny said. "Most folks are in bed—and Mohegan's out of town. Nothing to worry about."

Rich apparently saw the other figures in the doorway. "Who's with you?"

"Just some friends," Johnny said. "Howie Fry, Lin Rawles, and Mac Taggart."

"Mac's there?" And he seemed surprised. But he turned back into the room and lit the lamp. "I'll get some clothes on. Make sure the curtains are drawn," he said.

When Rich returned he had pulled on his trousers, a shirt, and was wearing slippers. His hair was tousled from the pillow and his beard shadowed the lower part of his face.

He seemed nervous, too, but he made a show

of friendliness. "Might still be some coffee in the kitchen. We'll take a look."

"No, we'll skip the coffee," Johnny said. "Hate to bother you this late, but it couldn't be helped."

Rich frowned. "Damnit, Johnny. That's all right. You ought to know how I feel about you."

"I've turned out to be quite a wanted man."

"In a struggle like this, things get rather confused. But after it's all over, people take a new look at what happened. I believe a great many of the charges against you can be wiped out."

"If I get arrested, will you represent me?"

Rich didn't hesitate. "Without any question."

"Howie and Lin, too?"

"Certainly."

"Hasn't come to that, yet," Johnny said. "But there is something I'd like you to do."

"Just name it."

The bedroom door had opened slightly. Johnny sensed that someone was standing there, listening, and he knew it had to be Merth.

"What I want you to do," Johnny said slowly, "isn't really for me. In a way, it's a service for Ben Mohegan, the town of Georgia City, and three of the people who live here. As it happens, Gil Jourdan, Shem Kelley and Mrs. Temple have had to leave town rather suddenly. I want you to represent them."

Rich looked puzzled. "But why? I don't understand, Johnny."

"They don't want their property damaged."

"But who's going to—Johnny, what are you telling me."

"Just this," Johnny said. "The two saloons and the restaurant have been closed. They won't be reopened for some time."

Rich smoothed his hand over his hair. His eyes had narrowed and for a moment he was silent, apparently measuring the significance and meaning of what this meant. A scowl worked into his face and finally he spoke. "You're hitting at Mohegan."

"Could be," Johnny admitted.

"The saloons are closed. No place Mohegan's men can buy a drink; no place to spend their time when they're in town; no restaurant where they can eat."

"That's about it."

Rich shook his head. "Maybe it sounds good, but really, it isn't. Some of the men working for Mohegan are pretty rough characters. At least, with the saloons open, they kept off the streets. Now, what will they do? How about the women in town? It won't be safe to step outside."

"You've got a sheriff, Rich. If a man steps out of line, have Ashe throw him in jail."

"Ashe is as bad as Mohegan."

"Then maybe Georgia City ought to do something about it."

"You say the saloons are closed. Mohegan will open them."

"How?"

"Bust open the doors."

"Then we'll sue him."

"But the saloons will be open."

"Who will run them? Where will they get liquor? The two saloons here are empty. Sure Mohegan can reopen them. He can wagon in whiskey, but if he tries that in Jourdan's or Kelley's, we'll take him to court and it'll cost him his shirt. Then of course he's got to do something about feeding his men."

Rich started pacing the floor. He shot a look at Mac, then Lin, then Howie, but from their expressions he got no help. Mac, Lin, and Howie seemed to be enjoying themselves.

"This is going to sound wrong," Rich said finally. "I'm dead against Mohegan, but I've got to look at the entire picture. I've got to think about the wives and children of the men who live here. So far, Ben Mohegan has kept his men pretty well in line, but if they've got no saloons to go to, no restaurant where they can eat, anything might happen."

"That's why I want you to see him tomorrow, when he gets back to town," Johnny said.

"What can I do?"

"Warn him to do as he's done. Tell him to keep his men in line. It's one thing to fight me, but it's another if he takes any action against the town."

"*You* have," Rich said.

Johnny grinned. "Have I? Who says a town can't get along without a saloon. And if anyone here is hungry, most folks have a kitchen. There's even a kitchen in the house Mohegan took. It's small, and someone would have to do the cooking, but it could be done. Now, how about it, Rich? Will you represent Jourdan, Kelley, and Mrs. Temple?"

"They haven't asked me to," Rich said, and he seemed suddenly irritated. "I can do it, but it's irregular."

"Then be irregular," Johnny said. "Many thanks. Time we should be riding."

Rich half raised his hand. "Johnny, I can't ask you where you're going, but there's no place in the valley you'll be safe. Now if you rode south—"

Lin Rawles spoke up, and he sounded amused. "Why south? No one's bothered us in days. We been having an easy time."

"Sitting around, getting fat," Howie said. "You tell Mohegan he can't follow a trail worth sour apples."

"That's about it," Johnny said. "I know a hundred hideouts in the Pothole Hills. We're not worried."

"You just see Mohegan in the morning," Mac

Taggart said. "Do it for me, as a citizen who's interested in Georgia City."

They turned toward the door, and on the way, Johnny glanced again toward the bedroom. He caught a glimpse of Merth, back in the darkness, but she stayed there.

"What'll you be doing now?" Mac asked, as they huddled on Gilmore's porch.

Johnny smiled. "I think we'll drop in on Mohegan's men."

"That'll mean shooting."

"Always a chance of it, but maybe we can avoid it. I noticed the men who rode in a while ago. They entered a darkened house, just as though they belonged. We could try the same thing, light a lamp, and then cover the men inside. I've been in the house. Only one bedroom. Mohegan would have kept it for himself, but we'll check it. Most likely, the men are bunking on the floor of the front room. It's a big room. A dozen or more could sleep there."

"What'll you do with them?"

"We'll herd them into the sheriff's office, and leave them there. It won't accomplish much. Henry Ashe will set them free. But the indignity of such a thing will hurt Ben Mohegan. One of these days, Georgia City might stir itself enough to slap Mohegan down."

Mac watched from a distance as Johnny, Howie and Lin approached the house. Johnny was tense as he stepped up on the porch. If the men inside were asleep, he had nothing to worry about—but some men slept very lightly.

Johnny moved on to the door. He opened it, stepped inside, and made no attempt to be silent. Blundering straight ahead he ran into a chair, swore angrily under his breath, and reached for a match. Off to the side, a man woke up, and made a sleepy protest. "Why the hell do you have to make so much noise?"

Lin and Howie, by plan, had stopped just inside the door. Their guns were ready. Johnny shuck the match, but cupped it to shield his face. By the flickering light of the match he saw several figures sprawled on straw mattresses spread on the floor. Off to the far edge was a table, and on it a lamp. Johnny shook out the match. He walked on to the table, struck another match, and lit the lamp. Then swiftly, he headed toward the rear rooms. Lin and Howie could command the room here. Possibly, the bedroom had been reserved by Ben Mohegan. But he had to be sure of it.

Undoubtedly, when he was here, Mohegan used the bedroom. Tonight, however, another had borrowed the room. He was a thin, sharp-featured man, and he woke up instantly when Johnny lit the lamp. He reached for his gun, too, but he didn't draw it. Johnny's gun was leveled at his head.

“Who are you?” the man gasped. “You’re not—Johnny Lang! How the hell did you get in?”

“Walked in,” Johnny said. “Get up quickly. Unbuckle your gunbelt and leave it on the bed.”

He backed away a step as the man stood up. From the front room he could hear Howie’s voice, issuing orders. He had heard a few grumbling answers. Howie had Lin to help him, and the lamplight to show them the room, but they had five or six men to cover. He wanted to get back there as soon as he could.

The thin-faced man had left his gunbelt on the bed. He squinted at Johnny and said, “Damned if you’re not raising hell around here. I half wish I was on your side. ’Course, we’ll get you in the end.”

“But not tonight,” Johnny said. “Walk into the front room—with your hands above your head.”

“You’re making a mistake,” the man said. “You ought to shoot me. My name’s Kelso.”

“Met a friend of yours in prison,” Johnny said. “Cottonwood Watkins. He had a knife he had made out of a spoon handle.”

Kelso laughed softly. “That could be Cottonwood. Never one to quit.”

“But he did, Kelso. He knifed one of the guards. They hung him. Now, march into the next room.”

In the front room, Howie and Lin had full command. Six men, who had been sleeping a moment before, now were awake. They were on their feet, their arms in the air. As Johnny and Kelso entered, they were backing to the side wall.

"You can join the others," Johnny told Kelso. Then he raised his voice. "Listen, everyone. If you do as you are told, you'll be tied up, but no one will be hurt. In time, you'll get free. Or you can start a fight—and get hurt. Which will it be?"

"Tie us up," Kelso said. "If I jump into a fight, I want to get an even break."

Several of the men made blustering threats, but no one tried to break away. After the men's wrists had been tied, they were marched to the sheriff's office. It was locked, but Johnny forced the door.

Kelso had a few last words to offer. "You got a good horse, Lang?"

"One with four legs," Johnny answered.

"Makes no difference," Kelso said. "If you had the fastest horse in the country, I'd run you down. Up to now, you just been a name—but you're laughing at me. That's going to cost you your life."

"We've all got to die, someday," Johnny answered.

Mac Taggart had delayed his return home until he was sure there would be no trouble at Mohegan's. Then he had hurried, and by the time Johnny, Howie, and Lin got to his house, Mac and his wife had gotten together supplies for the three men.

"The food's in three packages, just in case you get separated," he explained. "Do you want to say anything about where you're going?"

"It's best if I don't," Johnny answered. "Anyhow, when a man's on the run, he isn't always sure of his direction."

"You mentioned the Pothole Hills to Rich Gilmore, was that wise?"

"It was intentional. I doubt if we'll head for the Potholes."

They left town, heading for Georgia Creek. They followed the creek upstream, but left it at a watering place where the fringing trees had been cleared away. "Where we headed?" Howie wondered aloud. "Back to the mountains?"

"Like to take a chance?" Johnny suggested.

"What we been doing?"

"This is even more risky. What do you know about the swamps south of the river?"

Howie reined up. "You ain't thinking about heading for the swamps. Man, there's places in those swamps that can swallow up a man and his horse—and a herd of cattle, too. Why they tell me—"

"But how much do you really know about it?"

"I know at least this," Howie said. "Mohegan would never figure we went there. Or anyone else."

"Ever been there."

"Never. Been past the big one, maybe a hundred times. I've heard Ben Mohegan's got a hunting lodge in there, somewhere, but he's had the time to test out the land. If a man rode in, blind, he'd have no chance."

"I've never been there," Lin said, "but if we could see where we were going, I'd risk it. And I doubt if any of Mohegan's men would follow us."

"Hell, I'll risk it, too," Howie said.

"We ought to get there by sunup," Johnny said. "Maybe we can spot the trail Mohegan used, and once we cut into the swamp, we'll test our way every step. I doubt if I'll like the swamp, but it's what Mac suggested—a hole we can pull in after us."

"Don't make it that bad," Lin said dryly. "I want to crawl out, one of these days."

They rode on, heading north, but slanting toward the Sandoval Mountains. As the pink clouds of the morning brightened the sky, they came in sight of the fenced swamp. From a distance it looked like a dense bramble, dark and forbidding, but through it here and there were wide open spaces which looked lush and green—ideal meadow spots. At closer range, however, the green would turn out to be a wiry, saw-grass, the edges sharp as a jagged knife. The earth below was watery and soft.

But a man could ride into that swamp and

not be lost. Mohegan had found a way, and somewhere in a sheltered thicket, he had built a hunting lodge. Now, as a matter of survival, they had to find it.

# XII

They cut inside the swamp fence at the river, then circled east, watching for anything which might be a trail to Mohegan's lodge. They were in luck. They didn't find a marked trail but Howie noticed a weather-stained blaze on one of the trees fringing the heavy underbrush, and, deeper in the tangling maze, they saw another blaze marking.

Nowhere could they see a trail, but the slashed cuts on the trees hadn't been put there by accident, and if the trail hadn't been used often, it was understandable that it couldn't be seen.

From the second blaze they found another, off to the left. By now, they had dismounted, and were leading their horses, testing the earth below their feet. At places they waded in water, ankle deep, but it got no worse than that. And at least, if nothing else, they were hidden from sight of the valley road and the surrounding rangeland.

It took an hour to walk a mile, but in that time they came to the edge of the underbrush, and now, straight ahead, was a marshy lake. Off to the side, under the trees, they could see the shape of a building, a low-roofed cabin: Mohegan's hunting lodge. There could be no question of what they had found. This was where Mohegan occasionally went duck hunting. From the condition of the trail, it hadn't been used for some time.

"So there it is," Howie said. "Always wondered what it was like."

He stepped toward it, still leading his horse, but in three more paces he was floundering in knee-deep water. He was sinking deeper when Lin and Johnny reached him and pulled him back.

Howie sat down. He pulled off his boots to empty them, and after that he shook his head soberly. "Might not have made it alone. This swamp is what I've always heard. We got in, all right. Hope we can get out."

"We'll map the trail," Johnny said. "Learn it. And if we have the time, we'll find another trail out—just in case we need it. Now, let's see if we can reach the lodge."

They made it with no more trouble. Once inside, they explored the lodge. Actually, it was little more than a rustic cabin, one large room, two sleeping rooms, and a large storage closet. Blankets had been stored in a trunk. In a nearby cabinet was canned food, a canister of sugar and another of coffee. Around the lodge was an area, possibly as much as three acres, where the ground was solid, and where the horses could be grazed.

"We couldn't ask for much more," Lin said. "We going to stay here for a time."

"Maybe a week," Johnny said.

• • •

For the next two days, no one went into the swamp hunting for them. Johnny, Lin and Howie learned the trail out, then explored further to find another way through the swamp. In this venture however, they weren't successful. This hunting lodge was on high, firm land. A dozen solid fingers reached into the marsh grass and into the deeper tangle of undergrowth around them, but none went very far.

The third day, late in the afternoon, they drew straws. Howie won, or lost, depending on the viewpoint. But Howie seemed pleased.

"We'll walk you out of the swamp, just after dusk," Johnny said. "Circle to the river, then wade your horse to the road. From there, stick to the road until you get near town. Leave your horse in the trees along Georgia Creek, and walk in from there. When you talk to Mac Taggart, pump him for every bit of information he has. Then get back here. Don't go downtown, and don't take any chances at all. We'll be watching for you at the edge of the swamp at dawn. If you get here earlier, wait for morning. Don't risk the trail alone in the dark."

"Ask about Syl and Dru," Lin suggested. "Find out if Mohegan's sent any men into the Sandoval Mountains."

"I'll ask everything I can remember," Howie promised.

After dark, Johnny and Lin walked Howie to the edge of the swamp, saw him leave, then returned to the lodge.

"Hope there's no word on the girls," Lin muttered. "If Mohegan's men find them, Syl's dead."

Johnny rolled and lit a cigaret. "You rather liked her, didn't you?"

"What if I did?"

"Just asking."

Lin was staring into the darkness, and his face had tightened. "I ain't defending her," he said slowly. "And I'm making no apologies for myself. I'm twenty-seven years old, and I've been around a little. Maybe I ought to know better than to fall in love with a girl like Syl, but what happened, happened. Nothing I could do about it."

"I scarcely know her," Johnny said. "But Dru said she liked her, if that means anything."

"She was one of nine kids," Lin said slowly. "Her father was a sod-buster in Kansas. When she was fifteen, she was sold to a man fifty years older than her, for two milch cows and a jug of whiskey. If I ever meet him, I'll horsewhip him."

"Such things happen."

"You mean it could be true. Hell, I know it was. Syl could have come up with a better story if she'd wanted to. One way she proved it was the scars on her back—old scars. The man who bought her used to beat her. She had new scars on her back, too—Ben Mohegan's."

"Mohegan likes to use a whip."

"I mean to kill him."

"No. He's mine, Lin."

"What's the difference if he dies?"

Johnny leaned back. "Why did she marry him?"

"She didn't," Lin said. "Syl and Ben Mohegan never were married. When Mohegan found her she was working as a dance hall girl in Las Cruces. You see, I'm not fooling myself about her. I know what she's been. Mohegan saw her, wanted her, and took her. He brought her here against her will, but by that time, she knew how to handle him, and she made no attempt to get away. He was crazy about her and Syl gave him hell. She teased him until she nearly drove him crazy. She would flirt with him, then turn cold. Sure he took her, whenever he wanted to, but she gave him no satisfaction. Then one night he beat her—whipped her with a strap until her back was bloody. She knew, after that, what was ahead. Some night, he would kill her. But before things could get as bad as that, you and Dru got in the picture."

"What would you like to do, Lin?"

"I want her to get away, safely."

"Would you go with her?"

"Sure. Why not? I'm no plaster saint myself, but that's not the point. Crazy as it sounds, I want her. I mean I want to marry her and settle down and raise a family. We might not make it. We might not be good for each other at all. But I'd like to try. Reckon I'm dreaming."

"A man's got to have dreams," Johnny said. "I had one when I hit the valley. It grew up while I was in prison. I'm afraid it's fading."

"Want to tell me about it?"

"Nothing much to it, Lin. I thought of getting out of prison and of going far away—up to the Oregon country. There's free land, open to entry. I thought I might find a place, forest land maybe, where the trees had to be cleared, and where there might be a stream. After I'd cleared the trees I could try farming, and maybe run a few head of cattle. And some day I might meet a girl who might like it there. But chiefly, it would be a pleasant place, no fighting, no trouble."

Howie Fry returned from Georgia City half-an-hour before dawn. Johnny and Lin were waiting for him at the edge of the swamp, and Howie seemed in good spirits. "Nothing to it," he said, referring to the trip to town. "Not even a smell of trouble."

"And the girls?" Lin asked.

"No word on them at all."

After breakfast, Howie made a more detailed report about what he had heard from Mac Taggart.

Ben Mohegan, Henry Ashe, and the posse

which had headed toward the flats had returned to town at midmorning, four days ago. The men bound and left in the sheriff's office were still there. Henry Ashe, of course, cut them free. Everybody then headed for Jourdan's. They found it closed. Kelley's was closed, too. By this time, tired, thirsty, and angry, they had broken inside—but they found nothing to drink.

By this time, someone reported the restaurant was closed, and the men marched up to Mohegan's, looking ready to shoot anyone. At that point, Rich Gilmore went to Mohegan's. He wasn't there very long. Afterward, Rich told Mac Taggart that he had laid it on the line to Mohegan, but what he actually said, Mac didn't know.

From that day, Mohegan's men cooked their own meals. They had liquor, too, since the second day. A man made a trip to Bradentown to bring in as many bottles as he could carry. But it wasn't the same as having a saloon to which they could go, where they could hang around and meet others, and order their own drinks.

"They still searching for us?" Johnny asked.

"Not as hard as they were," Howie said. "First of all, Mohegan had to send a crowd south to turn his cattle back from the fence we cut. They've just finished. But the search hasn't been dropped. As Mac heard it, Mohegan's got three men sweeping through the Pothole Hills, looking for some trace of us. He's got two men far up at the north end of the valley, and a third party scouring the foothills of the Sandoval Mountains above Ute Flats."

"I don't like that," Lin scowled. "I don't like it a bit."

"How about the other ranchers?" Johnny asked. "Those on Ute Flats and over on Crows' Bench. Any word of them, or of what they're planning."

"Mac says they're waiting to see what happens. Or maybe they're waiting for a federal marshal to show up. They wrote for one, but near as Mac knows, there hasn't been any answer."

"Now about Mohegan? Does he spend his time in town?"

"He has—since the night he chased toward Crows' Bench. Of course, if he gets word about where you've been seen, he might head out that way, with every man he could raise. But he would want to be sure the trail was fresh."

Johnny was silent for a moment, but finally he nodded. "We'll give him two more days, or maybe three."

"What for?" Lin asked.

"To give Mohegan a better chance to feel the pressure he's living under," Johnny said. "He's a man of action. If he wants something, he smashes ahead and gets it. He loves to run into opposition. We've given him opposition, I know, but we're ghosts. He can't pin us down. When he hits at us, we're not there. If we could slap him in the face, once more, then vanish, Mohegan would go crazy. If this keeps on, he'll destroy himself. That's the only way we can whip him. You and I and Howie can't take on Ben Mohegan and twenty hired fighters. We wouldn't last a minute."

"One bullet would drop him," Lin said flatly. "Just one."

"And what of us? What of Syl? She couldn't take over the ranch, since she and Mohegan weren't married. The ranch probably would go to Mohegan's nephew, Will Mohegan, or some other relative, and Mohegan's gunfighters would still be here. Dal Osborne, Kelso, Shadow Wells—men like that."

They waited three days, then, at Johnny's insistence, they waited two more days.

"You're just waiting on rain," Lin said impatiently, late in the afternoon of the fifth day. "And that's foolish. It may be another week until we get any rain."

"At least, it looks clear now," Johnny admitted.

"Howie made it to town and back in clear weather. Three of us could do it the same way."

Johnny shrugged. "Maybe."

"Then, when are we going?"

Johnny smiled. "How would it be if we left tonight, right after dark?"

"Now, that's more like it," Lin said.

• • •

They took the course Howie had followed, and shortly before eleven, left their horses in the trees along Georgia Creek. Then, they approached the town by foot. They didn't hurry. It wasn't at all impossible that Mohegan had posted guards at various points throughout the town.

Along the main street, or around Mohegan's, there might be guards, but on the way in, Johnny, Howie and Lin didn't go as far as the main street, and at least on their way to Mac Taggart's, they saw no movement in the shadows.

Mac answered their knock as though he had expected them. He admitted them to the kitchen, closed the door, then struck a match and lit the lamp. "Windows all been curtained tight," he said. "Coffee's on the stove, waiting. Looked for you sure, last night."

"I've been waiting for rain," Johnny admitted. "Finally gave up. How are things in town."

"Folks are waking up," Mac said. "One of Mohegan's men went to Cy Bellam's to get his gun fixed. Found it closed, and a sign reading that Cy had gone away on vacation. Barber shop closed up, two days ago. Barber's home, playing sick. Word's been passed around that Ed Romig is going to lock up tomorrow night. After that, don't know where Mohegan will buy his groceries."

"That could work a hardship on others," Johnny said.

"Neighbors will help neighbors, if we run low on food," Mac answered. "The point is this. Georgia City doesn't like what Ben Mohegan's doing. We're letting him know."

"Any other news?"

"Plenty," Mac said. "I've just started. The ranchers all around Mohegan's started invading his range two days ago. They drove their cattle down the slopes to the main basin. Mohegan hasn't been able to do anything about it, either. The man who drove the cattle onto Mohegan's land didn't stay with them. The men disappeared. Mohegan sent a crowd over toward Crows' Bench. The men ran into three herds which shouldn't have been where they were—but no men guarding them. Of course, Mohegan's men could have driven the cattle up the slope, but that takes time and a chuck-wagon crew. Besides, Mohegan wants most of his men here in town, just in case of trouble."

"How many men does he have in town?"

"A dozen, at least. Maybe fifteen. Mohegan posts guards at night, too. Or maybe he has to. To sleep fifteen in that house he's using would pack them like sardines."

Johnny nodded. What Mac had told him was encouraging. Every bit of pressure that could be brought against Mohegan would help. For years, Mohegan had had his way in Georgia City. It had been his town. It had been his valley.

But suddenly he was running into opposition.

"But all the news isn't good," Mac said.

Lin swung toward him, his face suddenly stiff. "You don't mean Syl—"

"Mohegan's wife? No, I haven't heard a word about her," Mac said. "What I was going to tell you was this. Two men came to town yesterday, late in the afternoon. They were after the doctor for Mrs. Macey, who hasn't been well, and they went only to the doctor's house, then meant to leave town. But someone saw them, recognized them as men who worked on the Bench, and as they started to leave, they were stopped by some of Mohegan's men. A fight started. Both were killed."

"And is that all—is that the end of the story?" Johnny asked.

"Did you expect more?"

"Don't we have a sheriff?"

"Henry Ashe. He said the two ranch hands started the fight. The men who did the killing claimed it was a matter of self-defense. Ashe agreed."

"Any more bad news?"

Mac was frowning. "I don't know whether this is important, or not. But Merth wants to see you. She says it's important."

Johnny shook his head. "I don't want to go there. I don't think Rich could be trusted."

"He's not home," Mac said. "Something took

him to Santa Fe. Since he wasn't on tonight's stage, he can't get back now until tomorrow."

Johnny looked curiously at Mac. "With things at this stage, I don't understand why Rich left. If Mohegan's using him, I'd think he'd want him here. Or could it be possible that he went to Santa Fe to bring back a federal marshal?"

"Could be, but I doubt it," Mac said. "Merth said it had something to do with Mohegan, but she didn't explain. She might, if she talked to you." He hesitated, then added, "Merth and her husband haven't been getting along. From the way she looks, it's rather serious."

Mac then offered to bring Merth to his place, so she could talk to Johnny.

# XIII

Merth must have hurried. At least, she didn't take the time to brush out her hair. It was still braided for the night. She didn't look as pretty as Johnny remembered, either. The skin of her face was too pale, her lips were too narrow, her eyes too deeply shadowed.

But she managed a smile as she entered the room and she spoke to Johnny, then Howie, and then looked hesitantly at Lin.

"Suppose we forget a couple things," Lin said, and put out his hand.

"Thank you, Lin," Merth answered. "I didn't look at you very honestly. I'm sorry."

Merth took a place at the table, across from Johnny and at Lin's side.

"Just to be safe, I think we ought to post a guard outside," Johnny said. "Who wants to volunteer?"

"No one does," Lin said. "But I'll handle it."

"Keep a look toward the main part of town," Johnny said.

Lin nodded and stepped outside. At the table there was an uncomfortable silence. Merth had been staring at the table. After a moment she raised her head, glanced at the others, and then spoke. "It's hard to get started. I don't know where to begin. And maybe this isn't important, but I thought it might be. Mr. Mohegan's been married only twice. The woman who ran away the other night, the one called Syl, was just living with him. They never were married."

This was no surprise to Johnny, but the others at the table looked startled.

"How did you learn about it?" Johnny asked.

"I do a good part of my husband's paper work," Merth said. "Just a few days ago, Mr. Mohegan made a new will. In it, he declared that he and Syl weren't married. He also insisted that Dru wasn't his daughter. He provided that in the event of his death, his estate should go to his nephew, Will Mohegan. But Rich says that the court will throw out that part of his will. Rich says that in the event of Mr. Mohegan's death, Dru and another sister can contest the will, and break it."

Johnny leaned forward. "Another sister? Who do you mean?"

"Mr. Mohegan's second wife had a daughter. She was born after the divorce, but Mr. Mohegan was the father. Rich says there is no question of it."

"Where does she live—this other daughter? In Santa Fe?"

"Yes. In Santa Fe."

"Mohegan doesn't know about her?"

"No. I'm sure he doesn't."

"How did Rich find out about it?"

"Rich learned about it entirely through accident. The second Mrs. Mohegan, now living in Santa Fe, made an application for a loan. In investigating her character, an attorney in Santa Fe wrote to Rich, and asked about her marriage here, and about the divorce. The letter mentioned a daughter. Later, in Santa Fe, Rich looked up the woman and her daughter. The woman was still bitter about Ben Mohegan, but she conceded that if anything ever happened to Mr. Mohegan, she would accept any kind of help in her daughter's name."

Johnny was silent for a moment. He didn't regret, now, that Merth had been brought here. What she had told him was damned interesting. Mohegan had made a will, denying Syl was his wife, and denying that Dru was his daughter. Syl was out of the picture, but not Dru. Her relationship to Mohegan could be easily established. *What would happen, however, if Dru was killed? Would the nephew get the estate? Not at all. The other daughter, the one in Santa Fe, could establish her claim. And with Rich advising her, where did that put him: right up in the driver's seat.*

"Merth," Johnny said, "how long has Rich known that Edith Brooks was really Dru Mohegan?"

She smiled wearily. "For a long time. I guessed who she was shortly after she arrived. Just to be sure, Rich made an investigation. Dru's bank draft came from Philadelphia. Rich wrote an attorney there and learned that a Drusilla Mohegan had converted her money to a bank draft, written in the name of Edith Brooks. So we were sure who she was."

"I wish that wasn't the truth," Johnny muttered.

He was thinking of the surprise attack at the line shack. Rich could have betrayed him in the cave in the Pothole Hills. Instead, he had arranged the meeting with Dru in the line shack, guessing that Johnny would go there. And in a flurry of shooting at the line shack, Dru might easily have been killed. *If that had happened, and if Mohegan was killed, Rich would have had clear sailing in the control of the Double M through the daughter in Santa Fe.*

Merth shifted restlessly in her chair. "I'm worried about Dru. I know, of course, that she's Mr. Mohegan's daughter, and in his heart he knows it—but just the same."

"She's in no danger right now," Howie said.

"But she is," Merth said. "Maybe I shouldn't tell you but—"

"But what?" Johnny asked sharply.

"Mr. Mohegan has found them," Merth said. "At least, from what I saw. I mean I was at Mrs. Rogers' tonight for supper, helping with the children. I had put them to bed, blew out the lamp, and was at the window. The Rogers live in the house behind the one Dru used to use—where Mr. Mohegan lives now. From the window you can see across the side yard. It was dark, but—"

Johnny stiffened. "Get to it, Merth. What did you see?"

"Three men and two women. They rode up behind Mr. Mohegan's house. The women were tied. I don't think they had been hurt, but one, I think it was Syl, was struggling as they carried her inside."

Johnny sank back, and for a moment he was silent, considering what this meant. How the two women had been caught wasn't important. It might have been accidental, or someone might have found a trail to the cabin in the mountains.

"It's good Lin isn't here," Howie muttered.

"We'll have to tell him," Johnny said. "But not at first. When Lin comes in, I don't want anyone here to mention what Merth saw."

"You can't do anything about it, anyhow," Mac said.

"But we've got to," Johnny said. "Particularly, we've got to do something about Syl—and don't say anything about what kind of woman she is."

"Damnit, I wouldn't," Mac said angrily. "All I'm thinking of is what you'll be running into. Maybe a dozen men, or more. What chance would you have?"

"We've got another job first," Johnny said. "And that's Henry Ashe. When we go after

Mohegan, I don't want to have the sheriff riding our neck."

"How will you handle him?"

Johnny grinned, and stood up. "I think it's time Henry Ashe resigned. Don't you?"

"Sure, but—"

"Then why don't we collect his resignation. Call in Lin. We'll talk about it for a minute."

As Mac went outside, Merth looked up at Johnny, her face working. She said, "Johnny—Johnny, I don't want you to—"

He shook his head. "Forget it, Merth. Don't get protective."

"But Johnny, how can you—"

His voice hardened. "If you want to worry—worry about Rich."

"Rich—but he's done nothing wrong."

"I hope you're right," Johnny said flatly.

He stood staring at her and the thought hit him that if he had married her, she would have had the right to worry about him. She seemed worried, and this should have given him some kind of feeling. But it didn't. The power she once had had was gone. Sitting there at the table, she was just another woman—not really very important to him.

Henry Ashe lived in a small frame house in the south of town. Johnny, Howie, Lin, and Mac approached the place cautiously. It was dark and no lights showed inside. No one hailed them as they gained the front porch.

Johnny stepped up to the door. He knocked heavily, knocked again, then called, "Sheriff! Wake up!" He hammered the door again.

After a few moments, they heard the sheriff's grumbling voice demanding who was there.

"Mohegan wants to see you, right away," Johnny answered, making his voice heavy.

"Get there, soon as I can," the sheriff said.

They waited for him, and after a few minutes the door opened and Henry Ashe stepped on the porch. He gasped when he saw the four figures on his porch with their guns covering him. He shot his arms above his head. He seemed unable to speak.

"We'll go back inside," Johnny suggested. "You go first, Lin. Light the lamp, then curtain the windows."

Henry Ashe recovered his speech after they got inside, but he didn't show much courage. His words came out in a husky voice. "What you want of me? It's Mohegan who—"

"We'll get to Mohegan," Johnny said. "Get your wife up, Sheriff."

"But she's gone to bed. She's—"

"Get her up. Have her put on a robe. Mac, take the sheriff to the bedroom door and listen to what he tells her. We want her here as a witness."

The sheriff could do nothing but what he had

been ordered. Mrs. Ashe got up and entered the front room. She was a small, tired-looking woman, and she seemed terrified. It seemed to shock her, too, that Mac was here.

"Mrs. Ashe, we don't intend to harm you," Johnny told her. "And we don't want to harm your husband. We came here tonight just to pick up your husband's resignation as sheriff. We want you to witness it. I know a resignation doesn't require a witness, but in this case, it might be wise."

The sheriff stiffened. "Who said I was resigning?"

"Aren't you?" Johnny asked. "Look around the room. Seems to me as though you were looking down the gun barrels of three desperate men. At such a time, it might be smart not to be sheriff. Think it over."

"You mean—I get a bullet if I don't resign."

"What do you think?"

Henry Ashe chewed his lips. He hesitated over his answer.

"You sign it," Mrs. Ashe said, her voice shaky. "Sign anything they ask."

"Won't be legal," the sheriff muttered.

"But it will," Johnny said. "Don't make any mistake about that. If you resign as sheriff, you're finished. Your wife will sign it as witness. And Mac Taggart will sign as witness. He'll take the paper and show it around town. Of course you can try to deny it, but if you do, something might happen to you."

"It's blackmail."

"Sure it is. But take a look at what kind of sheriff you've been. I was forced in a fight and I slightly wounded Will Mohegan. You hunted me three days. The other day, two of Carl Macey's riders came in to get the doctor. As they were riding out, Mohegan's men stopped them, and killed them. The men who murdered them weren't even arrested."

"The evidence proved—"

"The evidence proved that if you ride for Ben Mohegan, you can get away with murder. Time to resign, Ashe?"

The sheriff glanced at Mac. "How come you're with them?"

"You'll be surprised how many men feel just like I do," Mac said. "Test the way the wind is blowing. You're getting out easy, Henry."

"Can't stay around here, if I resign, and if Ben Mohegan—"

"That's up to you," Johnny said. "I'm getting tired of all the talk."

The sheriff took another look around the room. His shoulders slumped and he turned toward the desk, off to the side. There, he scribbled and signed a paper. It was a resignation. Mrs. Ashe signed as witness, then Mac Taggart. Mac put the paper in his pocket.

"Now, if you're smart, you'll take a trip," Mac said. "Ain't you got friends in Springerville?"

The sheriff nodded.

"Then go see them," Mac said. "And don't wait until morning to get started. Your wife will be safe here at home."

"I'll think about it," the sheriff mumbled.

Johnny went outside. He was joined by Howie and Lin. Inside, Mac Taggart was making sure the sheriff would leave, and was reassuring the sheriff's wife.

"That was too easy," Lin said. "Maybe it'll be a shock to Mohegan to lose the sheriff, but isn't there something else we can do?"

"Yes, we've got one more errand here in town," Johnny said soberly. "But we can't rush it. We'll have to wait until it starts to get light."

"Name it," Lin said.

Johnny stared off into the darkness. He spoke slowly, picking his words carefully. "I've been thinking about it, Lin. I'm not sure it'll work the way I hope it will, but it's the only plan I can come up with which might be successful. Some time, during the next three hours, we'll get five saddle horses and tie them west of the back of Mohegan's. Then, as it gets dark, you and Howie will creep toward Mohegan's kitchen door. I'll be in front. When it's light enough to see, I'll let Mohegan's guard catch a glance of me. Then I'll run up the street, and if I make a fight from up the street, most of Mohegan's men will charge after me. That's when you and Howie will go in the back."

Lin's voice had sharpened. "You said five horses. There's only three of us. Who are the horses for?"

"One for Syl. One for Dru."

"Why didn't you tell me?"

"I didn't know myself until we talked to Merth. You were outside, standing watch."

"When did Mohegan get them?"

"They were brought in just after dark."

Lin was silent for a moment. When he spoke his voice sounded flat. "Syl's dead by now. If we'd hit Mohegan's earlier."

"But we couldn't have, Lin. There might have been a dozen men inside. We would have had to shoot our way in, and in a gun fight in the darkness, we might even have shot the women. We can't lift a finger until it gets light."

"That's about the size of it," Howie said. "And who says it's all over for Syl. Let's wait and see what we find."

Mac Taggart came out on the porch. "The ex-sheriff is packing his stuff," he announced. "He'll be gone in an hour. And I don't think he'll be back. His wife'll finish the packing, put up her house for sale, and follow her husband. Now, what about Mohegan's?"

"We have to wait for dawn," Johnny answered.

• • •

They brought their horses from Georgia Creek and tied them behind a barn that was only a short run from Mohegan's. One of Mohegan's men was posted in front of the house, and another in the rear. As the sky finally began to grow light, Johnny had a final conference with Howie and Lin.

"We'll have to wait until it's fully light," Johnny said. "We've got to be able to see what we're doing. There's only one way we might succeed—and that's to pull most of Mohegan's men outside. I don't want you two to move a step toward the back of the house until you can't stand it any longer. That might be ten minutes—or even fifteen."

"How you going to last ten minutes—or fifteen," Lin asked.

"After I've been seen, I'll hole up in Romig's grocery and bust through the window. Then I'll go out the back way and hit through the stage yard. Plenty of cover there. I'll get to where we left our horses."

"At least, this ought to wake up the town," Howie said.

"Let me wake them up," Johnny said. "I'll use up several rounds of bullets—make a lot of noise. You two are the ones who will be hurting Mohegan. Get the two girls, and get away."

He circled back to the other side of the main

street. He had left Mac behind the sheriff's office. He wasn't there when Johnny got back, but a few minutes later he showed up with two extra guns in his pockets. He gave one of the revolvers to Johnny.

"You're to keep out of sight, Mac," Johnny ordered. "Get to the street near the seed store and fire your guns a few times, so Mohegan's men don't think I'm alone. Then get back. All we want to do is draw Mohegan's men outside so Howie and Lin can get away with the girls. . . .Too many guns against us to make a final stand."

"Yep, I get the picture," Mac nodded. "But don't wait too long to get away."

Johnny grinned. "I want to live as well as you do. It's getting lighter."

Mac looked up at the sky. "Fifteen minutes more."

"Or maybe half an hour," Johnny said. "Be seeing you, Mac."

He twisted away, headed toward the main street, and then stopped at the front corner of the hardware store. From there he could look on an angle toward Mohegan's. It was light enough, now, to see the guard posted in front of the house. The man was sitting on the porch steps, his rifle across his knees. His head sagged forward. He might have been dozing.

Johnny leaned forward. He took a look up the street. No one was in sight. No wagons, no horses. In some of the homes away from the main street, a few people might be up, but most of Georgia City still was asleep.

Backing away out of sight, Johnny had a final cigaret. He checked the extra gun Mac had given him, dropped it in his coat pocket, checked his holster gun, and then took another look at the sky. It was much brighter. He could see no clouds. It was going to be a clear, hot day, and if they got away to head for the swamp, the ride would be hard and uncomfortable.

Johnny finished his cigaret, dropped it, and then swung toward the street. As he came in sight of Mohegan's, he half expected the guard to sense his presence and look up. But the man didn't. Without much question, he was dozing.

Johnny moved up the middle of the street. When he was directly in front of Mohegan's he stopped and drew his gun. Now, it was important that he be recognized, so Johnny raised his voice. "Hey there, mister," he shouted. "Someone looking for me?"

The guard jerked up his head, then scrambled to his feet, raising his rifle. He spotted Johnny in the street and he screamed, "Ben! It's Johnny Lang. I've got him!"

But he was wrong about that. Before he could fire the rifle, Johnny's bullet smashed into his shoulder and knocked him off balance. He dropped the rifle as he fell.

The door of the house jerked open and a man showed up against the dark background of the room. Johnny had been expecting something like that. He fired at the figure. Then swinging away he started running up the street. He hadn't taken three steps before a bullet from the house screamed past him.

Johnny looked back. He had heard a window breaking and now he saw a rifle pointing through the shattered glass. He fired a shot that way, put another through the open doorway, then hit the other window. That was enough for the moment. He had announced his presence quite effectively. If he stayed out there on the street, however, he wouldn't last very long. Moving up the street he headed for Romig's store. He nearly didn't make it. Shots again whistled past his head. One grazed his neck. Another tugged at the shoulder of his coat.

From the corner of the building next to the grocery, he caught a glimpse of Mac Taggart. He was firing steadily, aiming at Mohegan's, and as he emptied one gun, he reached for another.

Johnny glanced back again as he reached the grocery. And what he had wanted was happening. Or at least, part of it. Three men had burst from Mohegan's and were racing for cover across the street. Johnny held his fire, and two more men showed up in sight. Then two more. One, from his build, might have been Kelso. Johnny threw a shot at him, but knew that he had missed.

Johnny continued running and cut on toward the grocery store. He lunged against the window, then as the glass broke, he climbed inside. From the edge of the frame he looked down the street. Ben Mohegan himself had finally stepped outside, and with more of his men. He was shouting orders to his men, organizing the fight. And there was a possibility—a good possibility—that no one was guarding the interior of the house.

Johnny took a quick shot at the men down the street—just to let them know where he was. The men around Mohegan were splitting away, several hunting for cover to hold the front of the grocery. The men Johnny couldn't see undoubtedly were hurrying toward the rear of the grocery. In a few more minutes the building would be surrounded. He was being rushed more than he had planned.

He raced to the back door, unbolted it, and looked out. At first he saw no one, and he stepped forward, meaning to cut across the stage-office yard. But suddenly he couldn't. A man came around the corner of the building to block his way, and Johnny recognized him instantly. It was Kelso. How he had got here so quickly was hard to understand. And Kelso, probably, was as surprised as Johnny.

For just an instant they faced each other—

an instant of realization. Then Kelso clawed up his gun. He might have been terribly fast but Johnny's gun was in his hand, and all he had to do was tilt it level and fire. The shock of his bullet twisted Kelso half around. He fell against the corner of the building and sagged to the ground.

He was badly hurt, but still conscious. He stared up at Johnny, and spoke, the words scarcely audible, "Hell with you, Lang. In a fair fight . . ."

"You grabbed for your gun, Kelso," Johnny said. "What did you expect me to do?"

Kelso tried to speak again, but couldn't. He slumped sideways. Blood trickled from his mouth.

Johnny straightened. He took another step forward, but then stopped. Several other men were racing up the passageway Kelso had used. He could hear them clearly. They were so close that Johnny had no chance at all of reaching the protection of the wagons in the rear of the stage office. Backing away, he reentered the store, closed the door, and bolted it. He was pinned right here in Ed Romig's store, with Mohegan's crowd all around him.

He could hold his place for a time. He could guard the windows and the doors as long as his ammunition held out, and as long as a chance shot didn't hit him. But the end was a foregone conclusion.

Johnny moved to the middle of the store, then angled to the side and climbed behind a counter. He had heard men trying the back door, but they had stopped. And rather strangely, he could see no one at the front windows. Surely, by now, some of Mohegan's men should have been trying to break in.

There had been a scattering of gunfire when he had fled up the street. Then, for a time, there had been no shooting. Now it started again, but not in the way he had expected. The gunfire he heard came from down the street—and not only a few shots. From the sounds he could hear, it was a real battle. He could hear men shouting, screaming, cursing. He jerked to his feet, vaulted the counter, and started toward the front of the store.

He could easily guess what had happened. Howie and Lin hadn't managed to escape with the girls. Ben Mohegan must have learned what they were trying. He had turned back, summoning his men, and he had trapped Howie and Lin in the house. They were putting up a fight, of course, but against Mohegan's crowd, they didn't have a chance.

Johnny reached the front of the store. He peered through the window. Down the street toward Mohegan's he could see several huddled figures lying motionlessly on the ground. The firing, suddenly, had slackened. Then it stopped.

And as he stood watching he saw three men step into sight, their arms stretched above their heads. An instant later, he saw more men—at least a dozen. They came from both sides of the street, most carrying rifles. *And they weren't Mohegan's men!* Several, Johnny recognized. One was Ed Romig, who owned this store. Another was Anton Verducci, the barber, who was supposed to be home, too sick to work. Another was Mac Taggart—and that gave Johnny a key to what had happened. At some time during the night when he had been busy with Howie and Lin, Mac Taggart had found the chance to see some of the men here in town, had told them what was planned, and had summoned them to help if necessary.

Johnny climbed outside and as he turned down the street, Mac Taggart met him. He looked very well pleased with himself. "Had to do it, Johnny," he said defensively. "After all, we folks who live here have a stake in what happens. Been putting up with Ben Mohegan much too long. This seemed to be a good time to settle things up."

"Where is Mohegan?" Johnny asked.

"Back there, next to the sheriff's office. Someone brought him down. Don't know how badly he's been hurt. Find out when I can."

"Howie and Lin?"

"Don't think they've been hurt. Sent a man to stop them from running."

Johnny glanced up and down the street. It was hard to realize he could stand out on the street like this and not worry about himself. The three men who had surrendered were being marched toward the jail. Out on the porch in front of Mohegan's, Johnny saw Howie Fry. He started that way, then stopped, and said, "Mac, tell your men to be careful. I know that some of Mohegan's men have thrown in their guns. Some are dead or wounded. But two or three might have crawled in a hole. Be on guard against them."

"We'll ferret them out," Mac said.

Johnny headed on down the street toward Mohegan's. On the way he passed one of the motionless figures on the ground, and stopped briefly, recognizing the man. It was Shadow Wells. In a gun duel with someone else, his guns were swift and deadly, but that hadn't helped him in the closing minutes of the fight this morning. In a struggle between two groups, he had been just another man—one to be shot down. A bullet had smashed through his forehead.

Howie walked to meet him, and he was hurrying. "You better go in there and see Lin. Maybe Ben Mohegan's already dead, but if he isn't—"

Johnny straightened. "What do you mean? Is Syl—"

"Go inside and take a look at her face. When you do, maybe you'll want to do what Lin wants."

Johnny marched on. Inside the house and at the

bedroom door, he ran into Lin Rawles, who was checking his gun. He was pale and tight-lipped. His eyes looked wild. He said, "Johnny, where is he? What's happened to Mohegan?"

"He's been shot," Johnny said. "Maybe he's dead."

"If he isn't, he's going to be dead as soon as I reach him."

"That won't help Syl."

"It'll help me. Damnit, Johnny—take a look at what he did."

In the next room, Syl lay on the bed. Her face was puffed and swollen. There were scratches across her cheeks and forehead. She lay on her side, moaning. Her back was bloody from the cuts of a strap.

"Now, show me Mohegan," Lin said harshly.

"It's more important to get the doctor," Johnny said. "Mohegan will keep—if he's alive. Howie, find the doctor and bring him here. Find out about Mohegan, too."

Howie nodded and hurried away and Johnny glanced around the room. "Where's Dru?"

"Dru?" Lin said. "She wasn't here."

"What happened to her?"

Lin shook his head. "Search me. We had to knock over a guard before we broke in, then Howie got another man in the front room. But we didn't see anything of Dru. It's a cinch she wasn't here when we walked in."

Johnny took another look around the room. He glanced in the kitchen, then he looked in the cellar. Definitely, Dru wasn't here. But according to what Merth had seen, two women had been brought inside.

Lin was sitting on the edge of the bed, holding one of Syl's hands. He stooped over and whispered her name. She answered something, but Johnny couldn't catch her words. He stepped closer and said, "Lin, ask her about Dru?"

"No use," Lin said. "I think she knows who I am, but she can't say anything I can understand. Maybe when she feels better I can ask her. Where the hell is the doctor?"

"He'll get here," Johnny said. "He's probably been busy."

He walked to the front room and looked out in the street. Over at the feed store, the man who owned it was sweeping the porch. Two other men walked past, waved to him, then continued on their way. Through the morning air Johnny could hear the sound of the smithy's forge. In spite of all that had happened, the town was falling into its habitual patterns.

# XIV

Howie came back with the doctor, and then made a report on what had happened. Ben Mohegan had suffered only a scalp wound. It had been deep and he was still unconscious. But without much question he would recover. He had been carried to the doctor's house with four other men—all badly wounded. Five of Mohegan's men were in jail, five had been killed. The others had fled, and probably were on their way out of the valley.

"Has anyone seen Dru?"

"Not so far as I know," Howie replied. "Could Merth have been wrong. Maybe Dru is still in the cabin in the mountains."

That was possible, of course, but Merth had been very definite in what she had said. She had seen two women brought to Mohegan's. If one had been Syl, the other, almost certainly, had to be Dru. But then, what had happened to her?

"Mac has taken a temporary appointment as sheriff," Howie reported. "He says they'll hold Mohegan for trial, but I'm not at all sure of that. When folks learn what happened to Syl there might be a necktie party."

The doctor left the bedroom. He had a few uncomplimentary remarks to make about Mohegan, then he spoke about Syl. In another day she would feel a great deal better. Her back would be scarred, but the swelling in her face would go down, and eventually, she would look as well as before. In view of the beating she had taken, the doctor thought she had been lucky. A few heavier blows, and she might have died.

"When can she talk?" Johnny asked.

"She was talking to Lin when I left," the doctor answered.

He hurried on to the door, and as he left, Lin showed up. He looked calmer. The doctor's reassurance about Syl had steadied him.

"She's dropped off to sleep," he told them. "But she won't sleep very long. When she moves, the cuts on her back will wake her. I haven't forgotten about Mohegan, but for a time, I'm going to stay right here and look after her. And to hell with what folks say."

"Did she say anything about Dru?"

"Yes. Late last night, Mohegan sent her away with Dal Osborne."

"Where?"

"Johnny, I don't know. Syl couldn't tell me, but I can make a guess. Mohegan couldn't have sent her to the ranch. Nothing there. He couldn't have sent her any place here in town. No friends he could depend on. That leaves only one place left."

"The hunting lodge. Do you think Osborne might have known the way?"

"He could have, Johnny. He was top hand."

"What do you know about him?"

Lin shook his head. "Nothing good. He was a gunslinger, as well known as Kelso or Shadow Wells. Worse than that, he was a copy of Ben Mohegan. He's got the most ugly laugh I ever heard."

Howie agreed. "He's a mean one. No question about that. Makes me damned uneasy about Dru. Maybe we ought to get back to the swamp—fast as we can ride."

"You get the horses," Johnny said. "Two horses. Lin will have to stay here with Syl."

Howie brought two horses, and a few minutes later they left town, striking northwest across country. The sun was up and it was warm. After an hour they stopped briefly to rest their horses, and Howie spoke. "After we get Dru, what will you do, Johnny?"

"Ride on, probably."

"Oregon?"

"In that direction. I might get as far as Oregon. Who knows?"

"You know my ranch, don't you? It's not a bad place. Make a fair income. Get along with two men. Sometimes hire a third. Never got married. Reckon you know that."

"Never knew why."

" 'Tain't important. What I'm driving at is this. Why shouldn't I take a partner? Split the work and split the profit. We could get along, you and me. Now and then I like to go away, raise a little hell, then come back. Most of my meanness, I work out on such trips. You could do as you pleased. Even get married. Wouldn't bother me at all. Why do you have to ride away somewhere? This is a nice country, right here!"

"Thanks, Howie," Johnny said, "I know you mean it and I wish I could say yes. But it wouldn't be wise. What's happened here has given me a bad taste in my mouth. Nothing to do but go away."

"Then, come back some day."

"Now, I might do that," Johnny said. But he didn't think he would.

They rode on again. As they came to the edge of the swamp and found the trail to the hunting lodge, they stopped briefly and studied the ground. From the hoofprints they could find, two horses had proceeded them. And from the signs they could read, neither had returned.

"We'll be a little careful, moving in," Johnny said. "Leave our horses part way in, and then walk. And keep our guns handy."

Halfway to the hunting lodge they dismounted, tied their horses, and then crept forward. A few minutes later, and from the protection of a screen of shrubbery, they stared at the lodge and the surrounding area. Two horses were tied under the trees, but Osborne and Dru weren't in sight.

That meant they had to be inside the building.

"Someone's got to reach that lodge," Howie said, making his own judgment of the situation. "I'll take a chance on making it. Cover me, Johnny."

Johnny swung toward him. "No. Wait a minute, Howie. Howie—"

"Can't wait," Howie said. "Cover me, if you can."

He stood up and started for the lodge, running and he was halfway there when Osborne showed up at the door. He must have seen Howie coming and when he appeared his gun was in his hand. Howie stopped, raised his gun, but Osborne's shot came first and it jerked Howie half-around, slamming him to the ground.

Johnny stood up. His aim was deliberate, careful, and he fired twice. Dal Osborne fell against the door frame. He hung there for a moment, then slid down on his knees. He then made an attempt to get up, but Johnny, aware of Howie's huddled figure, fired again. The man in the doorway jerked as the bullet hit him. He pitched back into the room, rolled on his face, and didn't move again.

There was a bullet wound in Howie's side. It was bleeding heavily, but it could have been worse. Johnny took off his coat, ripped up his shirt, and made an emergency pack. He tied it in place over the wound.

Johnny then looked toward the lodge. In spite of the shooting and in spite of the figure lying in the door, Dru hadn't come in sight.

He walked toward the door and when he got there he prodded Osborne's body with his boot. The man gave no response. Johnny stepped across him and entered the room beyond. Dru wasn't anywhere in sight. He turned to the side and in one of the sleeping alcoves he found her.

Dru was lying on the bed. She wasn't bound and at first Johnny thought she was dead. But she wasn't. And she wasn't unconscious, although she might as well have been. Her eyes were wide open, but glazed and vacant.

What had happened wasn't hard to imagine. Osborne had been rough with her and from the scratches on her face and body, she had fought back. But it had been useless. She had been no match against Osborne's greater strength.

Johnny spoke to her. "Dru. Dru, it's Johnny. Nothing to worry about now. Osborne's gone."

She didn't answer, didn't give any indication she had heard.

"Dru," Johnny said, leaning toward her. "Dru, look at me."

She still didn't answer.

Johnny found a blanket, covered her, then turned away. He looked in the other sleeping alcove, stripped away the top blankets to use as a cover for Howie, then went outside. And as he passed Osborne's body a sudden flash of anger hit him. He kicked the dead body in the door, kicked it again and swore. But that didn't help a bit. Only time would erase the memory.

Johnny carried Howie, who was still conscious, inside. He found a better bandage to pack the wound, tied it in place, then took another look at Dru. She hadn't moved. She still seemed unaware of where she was. Johnny spoke to her again, but she didn't answer.

He stooped over, slipped his arm behind her shoulders and pulled her up. He shook her and said, "Dru. Dru, listen to me. Howie's been hurt. You've got to help me."

She had stiffened momentarily and she tried to twist away. Her words came in a mumble. "Leave me alone. Don't touch me."

Johnny shook her again, then he slapped her sharply across the face. "Dru! Wake up. Damnit, I need your help."

Tears welled in her eyes and she rolled away. Johnny let her go. He straightened and stood looking down at her. Suddenly, she was crying, crying so hard her body shook.

"All right, go ahead," Johnny said harshly. "But get your crying over. Did you hear what I said a moment ago? Howie has been wounded. I need your help."

She kept on crying, and in another moment Johnny left her. In the main room he built up the fire in the stove and started water to boiling. Then, he pulled Osborne's body outside, so the door could be closed. Back inside the house he started to fix something to eat and was standing at the stove when he heard a sound from the alcoves. Looking around, he saw Dru. She had dressed and she looked terribly pale, but she stood stiffly erect.

"Where's Howie?" she asked.

"In the other alcove," Johnny said.

Dru turned that way and disappeared from sight. Johnny started to follow her, then changed his mind. A few minutes later, Dru reappeared.

"His wound ought to be cleaned," she told him, and she was trying to keep her voice steady. "Do we have any hot water?"

"It's getting hot," Johnny said.

"Howie ought to be seen by the doctor. I don't suppose there's any chance of that."

"I'll ride for the doctor if you can look after him."

She bit her lips. "The man who was here . . ."

"He's dead."

"That doesn't change things, does it?"

"Nothing in the past ever changes. But what of that? What counts is the way we look at things. What happened here wasn't important. It might have been ugly, but if that's the worst thing that ever hits you, you'll be lucky."

She took a deep breath. "What could be worse?"

"A hundred things I could mention," Johnny said. "To go blind, to be permanently injured, to be killed. Or to lose a husband or a child, or to hurt someone you loved. It's time to do some honest thinking, Dru."

She showed a faint interest. "What happened to Ben Mohegan."

"He's under arrest."

"That's not enough. I'd like to see him dragged by wild horses. I'd like to use a whip on him. I'd like to—"

"Hey—slow down," Johnny interrupted. "You really don't mean it, Dru. You can't."

"But I do."

Johnny pushed his chair back. He rolled and lit a cigaret. "I'm going after the doctor," he told her. "I don't think Howie's wound is too serious, but I don't want to take a chance. Can you look after him until I get back?"

"I can look after him. What about Syl?"

"She didn't have an easy time, but she's all right now. Lin's with her."

He got up, took a look at Howie who was sleeping, then went outside and headed for the trail through the marsh. They had left their horses some distance away. Johnny decided to bring Howie's back to the lodge before heading for town. Then he started thinking about Rich Gilmore. He had to do something about Rich, but what course he should follow he didn't know.

Johnny was puzzling about him as he passed the screen of shrubbery from which he and Howie had peered toward the lodge. He heard a sound, and sensed the presence of a man's figure moving toward him. He jerked that way, and in the split second which followed, he saw and recognized the man: Ben Mohegan! A wide bandage circled his head. Below it, his face looked ashen and was deeply lined. The doctor had told him that Mohegan had suffered a serious scalp wound, but it couldn't have been too bad. At least, in some way or other, the man had escaped from the doctor's house, had found a horse, and had fled. Following such a trip, he should have been ready to collapse. Instead, the charge of his body carried Johnny off his feet.

Johnny had grabbed his gun, but before he could lift it, Mohegan's powerful arms closed around him and pinned them down. They hit the ground with Mohegan on top. He had switched his attack to get Johnny's gun, and for half-a-minute they struggled for it. Mohegan was noisy about it, too. He had a bellowing voice and he used it, shouting his profanity.

In the battle for the gun, Mohegan rolled away. Johnny got up on his knees. He dropped the gun, but as Mohegan reached for it, Johnny hit him sideways. In the scramble to get the weapon, his arm brushed the gun. It skidded into a pool of water and disappeared.

A scream of disappointment broke from Mohegan's throat and a slamming fist scraped the side of Johnny's face. Johnny stabbed a blow in return, backed away, and scrambled to his feet. But as quickly as he did, Mohegan reared to his feet, then lunged straight ahead.

Johnny covered up, taking Mohegan's blows on his arms and shoulders. He stepped sideways and felt himself splashing in the soggy earth of the marsh. He drove forward to solid ground and ripped another blow at Mohegan's face. But Johnny ran into a solid fist which caught him on the side of the head. That was followed by another and another. His knees buckled and he sank to the ground. A knee smashed into his face and he rolled sideways. Then, because he knew he had to, he struggled to his feet.

His vision was blurred, but he could see Mohegan rocking toward him. Johnny brought up his fist, swinging his body with the blow. He jabbed with his other arm and Mohegan blundered past him, staggering. Something tripped him. He splashed into the marsh waters. He got up, staggered on, then fell once more.

Johnny gulped for air. He was dizzy. He knew he was swaying from side to side. If Mohegan had been right here he doubted if he could defend himself. But for the moment he wouldn't have to. Mohegan had staggered from the trail. He had fallen in the swamp, had climbed to his feet, and then had plunged farther away. He was now sitting up again, waist-deep in the muddy water.

"You better come back here," Johnny called. And then he spoke louder. "Mohegan—it's not safe out there. You better get back to the trail."

The man looked around, his expression still ugly. "Hell with you, Lang. I'll be back. This is where you'll end."

He started struggling but he couldn't get to his feet. Instead, he sank deeper in the sucking mud. He tried again; he was screaming with the effort he was making. But it didn't help. He was now arm-pit deep, and he looked around at Johnny with a shocked, terrified expression on his face. "Lang!" he shouted. "Lang! It's caught me. I can't get free. Get some branches."

Johnny glanced from side to side. He could see no broken off branches along the trail. Off to the side, several yards away, was one. Johnny stepped toward it, but he sank knee-deep in the mud and had to pull back.

Suddenly, Dru was at his side. She grabbed his arm and shook him. Her voice was a scream. "Johnny, you've got to do something. You can't leave him there. Johnny! Did you hear me. If you don't—"

She jerked away and plunged toward Ben Mohegan. But she couldn't reach him. The mud caught her before she was halfway there. Her skirt billowed around her and seemed to hold her where she was.

Johnny reached her. He grabbed her around the waist and started pulling her back to the trail. Dru was fighting him, trying to get free to help her father. Johnny took a quick glance at Ben Mohegan. He had sunk deeper in the mud. Now only his head, his arms, and the tops of his shoulders were in sight.

He was still shouting, begging, and he had recognized Dru! "Drusilla—Drusilla—you can't leave me here. I'm your father. Drusilla . . ."

He flailed his arms in the air and the effort pulled him even deeper. The mud and the water now came to his chin. He was screaming, and the sounds were weighted with a horrible fear. Dru stared at him and a shudder ran over her body. She collapsed in Johnny's arms. She turned her head and buried her face against his chest. As Johnny pulled her back to the trail, the screaming stopped.

Johnny lowered the girl to the ground. He sat beside her. He was still short of breath and shaky and sore in every muscle. There was a swelling below one eye which nearly closed it. His lower lip was cut inside, and had puffed up. His arms ached from the blows he had taken. Peering into the swamp he looked at the place where Ben Mohegan had disappeared. The wiry reeds at that point were thinner and some were broken, but he could see no other signs of what had happened.

Dru stirred. She sat up, but didn't look into the swamp. Her voice sounded tired. "He's gone, isn't he?"

"Yes, Ben Mohegan's gone," Johnny said. "It wasn't an easy death." His voice had sharpened. "He died the way you wanted."

"You don't have to remind me," Dru said. "I'll hear those screams as long as I live."

Johnny was silent for a moment, but finally he said, "Dru, in the final minutes, you tried to reach him. That's one thing to remember."

"But I couldn't."

"*We* couldn't."

Johnny Lang spent a week in Georgia City. He waited until he was sure Howie was well on the way to a complete recovery. He stood up as best man when Lin Rawles and Sylvia Ackerman were married, then bid them farewell when they left by stage.

One unpleasant job still faced him. In a meeting with Rich Gilmore, he had been brutally honest in his suspicions. Of course he couldn't prove that Rich had hoped Dru would be killed at the line shack, or that through the other Mohegan heir, he had planned to control the valley. But the rumor of such a plan got around, and Rich Gilmore decided to move to Sante Fe. Merth went with him. Perhaps, in Sante Fe, she and

Rich would make a better life for themselves.

The invading herds, owned by the ranchers fringing the valley, were withdrawn from the Mohegan property. The old roads were reopened. And Dru, acting for herself and her half-sister in Santa Fe, took active charge of the Double M ranch.

"I wish you'd stay and run it," she said to Johnny.

"Nope. It'll keep you busy."

"You think that'll be good for me."

He grinned at her. "Won't it, Dru?"

"What will you do?"

He was silent for a moment. It hit him abruptly that he could stay here, with Dru, and it was a tempting thing not to. Mac Taggart, acting as sheriff, had cleared his record. He had good friends here in the valley. And as for Dru—she might become quite a person.

"Johnny, what will you do?" she asked again.

He looked away, scowling. "I'll go away, Dru. I have to. I didn't want a part in the struggle here in the valley. I think I'll go to Oregon—just as I planned. That is—I will if I don't get terribly lonely. . . . That might happen."

She touched his arm. "I hope you do."

He suddenly leaned toward her, raised his hands to her shoulders, and kissed her. It made him want to forget about Oregon, but he broke away after a moment and stepped back.

“I’ll be waiting,” Dru said.

“You do that,” Johnny said.

He swung away and walked toward his horse, but his step was light. He doubted very much that he would go as far as Oregon.

**Center Point Large Print**
600 Brooks Road / PO Box 1
Thorndike, ME 04986-0001 USA

**(207) 568-3717**

**US & Canada:**
**1 800 929-9108**
**www.centerpointlargeprint.com**